Western

DATE DUE			
3-16	4-21		
4-8	5-25		
5-19	10-9		
6-22	2-15		
10-11	4-14		
11-20	12-30-13		
2-9	6-17-21		
11-7			
3-17			
12-4			
12-20			
3-24			

F   Dearen, Patrick.
DEA
        When cowboys die

WHEN COWBOYS DIE

PATRICK DEAREN

M. EVANS AND COMPANY, INC.
NEW YORK

M. Evans and Company, Inc.
216 East 49th Street
New York, New York 10017

Library of Congress Cataloging-in-Publication Data

Dearen, Patrick.
    When cowboys die / Patrick Dearen. — 1st ed.
      p. cm. — (An Evans novel of the West)
    ISBN 0-87131-756-7 (cloth) : $18.95
    1. Cowboys—Texas—History—20th century—Fiction.
I. Title. II. Series.
PS3554.E1752W44   1994
813'.54—dc20

                                          94-785
                                           CIP

Typeset by Classic Type, Inc.

Manufactured in the United States of America

First Edition

9 8 7 6 5 4 3 2 1

For Wesley, My Partner

Chapter One

The cowboy boots were dusty and well-worn, the pointed toes as scuffed as an old cattle trail and the cowhide uppers strangely split down the front.

From the outlying pen, the Mexican ranch hand noted the odd lacing as the big stranger approached from the chalky road that fronted the remote line-camp shack in the mesquites and cedars. The illegal alien lifted his eyes up along the thread-bare jeans and the puddle of sweat darkening the western work shirt. Rolled-up sleeves bared swarthy upper arms and tattoos—*Texas* on the left, *Roper* on the right. He found the leathery face and stubble, the crow's feet marking the eyes, the brim of the sweat-stained Resistol throwing a shadow across bulging veins in the temples.

But it was the corroded, bolt-action .22 rifle, dangling from a glistening hand, that dominated.

Charlie Lyles rounded the back corner of the sagging shack and squinted at the sudden glare of evening sunlight from left-side mesquites bunched like cattle in roundup. A mirror-like pickup at a shed, it was a reminder he didn't need. The pungency of horse manure from the pen ahead was more to his liking, for it stirred so many memories of how a cowboy should live.

7

He smelled the boiling beans too, and saw the wetback, standing with arms folded across the top rail and puffing on a cigarette. Yet it was the long-maned bay with head buried in a grain trough that captured his attention most.

Nearing the Mexican, Charlie saw the eyes shaded by the straw hat meet his own, then grow close-set as they drifted down to the rifle. Even as the alien took his foot from the bottom rail and turned to him, the firearm remained the more powerful presence.

"Buenas tardes," Charlie said.

The only reply was the screech of a nearby windmill as the Mexican lifted, then lowered, penetrating eyes.

Charlie waited until he was within arm's reach before he stopped; he hoped to intimidate the Mexican purely with his greater stature—a six-foot, three-inch frame bearing a supple two hundred thirty pounds.

Still, the Mexican studied only the rifle; Charlie made sure he saw his fingers flexing just above the trigger guard.

The gelding looked up momentarily and nickered softly, catching Charlie's eye. Through the warped rails, he could see the wind ruffle the mane and the tail swish flies from a coat reddened by the West Texas sun. It was just the kind of cow horse Charlie liked—bright-eyed, lots of muscle, not too leggy.

"Good lookin' caballo you got there," he said quietly. He turned to the ranch hand only when he noticed him withdrawing a step.

"Señor McBee's," the Mexican said uneasily. "I work for him."

Charlie lowered his head and spat, the spittle catching the bottom rail and dribbling down. "Got a cigarette, amigo?" He again surveyed the horse—the broad breast, the shod hooves trampling the muck before the trough.

The Mexican cleared his throat nervously. "Sí, I have a cigarette." He produced an open pack from his shirt pocket, shook one out, and extended it.

Charlie turned, and for the first time they stood face-to-face. Charlie's bloodshot eyes met apprehensive ones. The Mexican's jaw trembled. The sweat of anticipation broke out on his forehead. And for long seconds they stared at one another, two men brought together at the same point in time, yet with an entire century separating them.

Charlie took the cigarette and hung it lazily in the corner of his mouth. He found a match in his jeans and struck it against the rusty rifle barrel. He looked up to find that the Mexican's eyes had followed the match to the firearm, and even after Charlie brought the flame on up to the cigarette, the alien's attention stayed fixed on the flexing fingers that left sweaty imprints against metal.

Charlie took a deep drag and glanced at the back screen door with the rag-stuffed holes. He could smell the beans again, and it set his stomach growling for something to fill its cavity besides knots. Food and water could satisfy that need, all right, and a good night's sleep his weariness, but the hollow that swelled in his spirit seemed unquenchable.

"Whatta you got to eat, compadre?" he asked.

The Mexican looked up and again withdrew a step. "I . . . don't think know you," he rasped. "You live town, 'round this place?"

Charlie flinched at thirty-two years of memories. "I ain't from nowhere," he snapped, and then his voice dropped. "Never was, don't guess." He nodded back toward the small overhang hiding the screen door from the sky. "You cookin' some beans? What else you got?"

"Sí, beans, bread, not too much." He looked directly into Charlie's eyes and shuddered visibly. "Maybe . . . maybe better you go."

Charlie's cheek twitched; he was sorry it had come to this. "No can do, compadre." And casually, as if without threat, the barrel of the rifle began to rise, from ground to Mexican work boots to dirty brown pants and cracked belt, until the muzzle swayed ever-so-slightly before the suddenly heaving chest.

"What-what you want?"

Charlie didn't wish to hurt the man; after all, the rifle wasn't even loaded, and anyway, he had worked with enough wets to know they made damned good hands sometimes. He just had to come across tough enough to intimidate him. "See that caballo over there?" Charlie asked, nodding to the pen. "I want you to get a saddle, throw it on him. Savvy?"

The Mexican stared at the rifle muzzle and another shudder passed through him. "Sí, I sabe. Me, I do good job, get saddle, fix horse up bueno."

"Get to doin' it then."

As the Mexican nervously turned and led Charlie past the bent-fendered pickup to the tack shed, it was Charlie's vision, not the rifle, that remained fixed on the ranch hand's shoulder blades, where sweat suddenly had soaked through the shirt. The rickety door, with nails half-withdrawn from the hinges, creaked inward, and through the shadows filtered the odor of grain and leather. Stopping at the threshold, Charlie planted a boot on the dirt floor and watched the Mexican hoist a blanket, bar-bit bridle, and grimy saddle slashed with cracks. Charlie reached for a frayed catch-rope hanging just inside the door, then backed away to let the man outside, the saddle catching splinters as it brushed the facing.

"Why hell you do this?" asked the Mexican as he went to the pen gate and swung it back on shaky hinges. He looked back at Charlie, who had taken a deep drag on the cigarette. "That horse, he good for nothing. Look, pickup. Drive bueno. So why hell?"

Charlie swallowed. He breathed deeply, tasting the horse sweat, the leather, the manure. He drew again on the cigarette and a gray column of ashes tumbled to his boot. "Why the hell not?" He glanced at the pickup, then nodded to the gelding. "Figure me and him got somethin' in common. Ain't neither one of us got much use in bein' here no more. Go on, buckle that kack on him, plenty pronto. Savvy?"

Inside the pen, the Mexican slipped the bridle on the bay and tied the reins to a fence post. Charlie stood nearby, taking in the web of shadows playing on the animal's rib cage. Turning, he traced the sunlight back through the limbs of a wind-blown mesquite and noted the low profile of the sun, sinking slowly into the brushy flats which fell away unseen into hidden canyons of the Colorado River watershed.

Almost tenderly, he nudged the Mexican in the ribs with the rifle muzzle as the man threw the blanket across the horse's withers. "You saddle that caballo up good, tie on this catch-rope, okay? Me, I'm steppin' in the house a minute. You let that horse get away, maybe this rifle'll go off. You savvy all that, compadre?"

Having flinched at the touch of the rifle, the Mexican now stood looking at him submissively, fear indwelling his eyes. "Sí, señor. I sabe bueno. I do bueno job for you."

Charlie lowered the rifle to carry it loosely back through the manure and out the gate. At the big rock serving as a back-door step, he reached for the screen's grimy handle and looked over his shoulder.

The Mexican's eyes had followed him all the way, but they quickly shifted to the saddle, which he hurriedly seized and threw across the gelding. "I fix him up, señor, have ready for you."

Charlie went inside. The kitchen was crudely furnished— battered table with uneven legs, a cane-bottom chair, and a rickety cupboard set against a smoked wall. He found a cankered spoon on the greasy stove and tasted the beans that gurgled over a butane fire. They were scorched and unseasoned, and like pebbles against his teeth.

Next to the kerosene lamp on the cupboard he found half a loaf of stale bread and canned goods—three pork and beans, two Vienna sausage, corn, and beef stew. In a drawer he came across a carpenter's cloth nail-sack, and when he dumped the contents, a pair of wire cutters and three boxes of .22 long rifle shells fell on the counter. Inspecting the yellow boxes to find neat rows of lead slugs, he slipped them into his shirt, then the wire cutters into his jeans. He packed the striped pouch with the food items and spotted a gallon milk jug on a shelf. It held just enough to whiten the bottom, and when he unscrewed the cap the odor of clabber turned his stomach. Emptying it in the sink, he listened to it gurgle down the drain, then he rinsed the jug and filled it with water from a cedar bucket.

Turning, he found spurs dangling from a nail and buckled them on. Starting outside, he paused at the table to reach for an almost-full carton of Camel cigarettes. His eye caught a few scribbled words in a crumpled letter underneath, and he knew enough Tex-Mex to see there was something about kids, a bunch of them, back home in Old Mexico. At least they had somebody who cared, even if he was way off up here in another country, struggling to make a few dollars to send them every month. Impulsively, Charlie dug in his jeans for the roll of ones next to the driver's license in his billfold and tossed it on the letter. Hell, what use did he have for money anymore?

Then he was outside again, the food pouch and water jug in one hand, the rifle in the other.

The saddle horse nickered. The Mexican stood holding it, and the animal bared its teeth at the bit and pranced at the length of the reins. Charlie came up before them, the rifle still carelessly at his side, and tied the pouch and jug to the saddle. He reached for the reins as brown hand lightly brushed his own, then the leather strips found his fingers.

"Okay, amigo, you go cook your beans now," he said, grasping the saddle horn.

The Mexican withdrew a step as Charlie dug his boot into the stirrup. "You no get 'way with this," said the alien, watching Charlie swing across the horse's withers with a creak of leather. "They come look for you, put you jail."

Charlie laid the rifle crossways before the saddle horn. He tossed his cigarette butt at the Mexican's feet, where it sizzled in the fresh manure. "Let 'em try," he snapped, all the submerged frustration surfacing as he reined the horse to the open gate. "You tell 'em, amigo, you tell 'em plenty. Just me, my horse, one forked rider and a rifle. Tell all those hombres with their fancy equipment to just stay out of my world or play hell tryin' to catch me."

He squeezed the horse with his thighs, and the Mexican and corral receded to the slap of hooves against dirt.

The bay was nervous, as if it sensed something unusual, and resisted the reins, its forelegs unsure. Charlie read the tightness building in the shoulders and kept it from downing its head; he liked a spirited horse, all right, but now wasn't the time. As he reached the bone-white lane cutting through greenery, a pack of cigarettes tumbled past his boot. He slowed long enough to secure the pouch, then the fence posts were bouncing alongside with the gelding's easy lope through the caliche dust.

A near-wilderness rose about him, filling him with strange exaltation now that he was astride a horse. There was barbed wire, all right, corralling the cedars, mesquites, and scrub oaks and skirting gullies of bleached limestone. But the air held sudden freedom, in every whiff of sun-baked cedar, in every gust that set the lacy mesquite leaves quaking.

Still, as he rode directly into the setting sun, voices swam through his head.

Turn back, Charlie. There's no place to run. You'll never get away on a horse.

He shook himself like a just-saddled bronc on a frosty morning.

I'm gonna make it.

Within a few minutes he struck a deserted, curving highway, crossed it as horseshoes pounded on pavement like heavy rocks, and followed the rusty fence line three hundred yards west through crackling broomweeds and yellowed grass.

Where a clump of scrub oaks and mesquites marked a fenced pasture corner, he pulled rein at a gate to bend over and unwire it.

We've got semi-automatic weapons, radio communica-
tion, jeeps, helicopters.

I'm gonna make it.

The support post sagged as he swung the gate inward a
horse's breadth. His jeans rasped against wood as the gelding
squeezed through. He stopped only long enough to reach
down and wire it shut, then he turned to the distant line of
dark green cedars marking the rim of slashing canyon lands.

Give it up, Charlie. We've got you beat. You can't get
away. Give it up and try to live like everybody else, try to
live in the nineteen nineties.

I'm gonna make it.

There's no place to run, Charlie, there's no place to run.

I'm gonna make it, damn you!

And by the time he was three horse lengths inside the
gate, he had the bay in a gallop, straight for the rocky,
cedar-shrouded canyons ahead.

Chapter Two

The cowboy boots were lustrous and still like new, a hand-made pair as unblemished from underslung heels to pointed toes as the coat of a just-foaled colt.

Folded across one another on a coffee table, they complemented the stylish brown jeans stretching to L. D. Hankins' chunky torso. He slouched on the sofa, his midriff sagging over the big silver belt buckle. Picking birthday cake coconut from his teeth and sipping Lone Star, he counted up his thirty-two years and felt a strange sense of loss. Time was escaping him; his *life* was escaping him. And there wasn't a damned thing he could do about it besides sit here putting on the pounds and think about all the big ideas of adolescence he had let get away.

Again, he thought of Charles Goodnight, riding across the Pecos desert in 1866 to help give birth to the mythical cowboy and a romanticized cattle trail. Seven hundred miles of wilderness. The threat of Comanches. Stampedes. Quicksand. Thirst, and more thirst. In L. D.'s younger days, he had yearned for such adventure, even expected it some day. But not only was he already two years older than Goodnight had been, he wondered if the world hadn't already seen its last real cowboy.

That is, except for one—and his name damned sure wasn't L. D.

"Sure looking glum to be your birthday, L. D."

He looked up to see Sarah come out of the kitchen. She was pretty, in a plain sort of way, the lamplight casting a soft glow on a face always without makeup. L. D. liked her that way—real and earthy, sandy hair unkempt but for a rubber band holding it in back. She had missed a lot of strands and her cheeks and lips were a little pale, but L. D. was still glad she didn't hide behind cosmetics or a perm or the latest clothing style. At least he knew that when he looked at her standing there in a simple cotton blouse smudged with flour and an apron wet with dishwater, he was seeing somebody real in an increasingly artificial world.

L. D. patted the couch beside him. "Why don't you leave that kitchen alone for a while, sit down, talk some. We don't hardly ever talk anymore."

She wiped her hands on her apron. "*You're* somebody to be complaining. You hadn't said ten words to me the whole time you been home. Didn't you like your birthday supper, darlin'?"

"Aw, come here," he said, patting the couch again. "Don't go gettin' your feelin's hurt. I just . . . aw, I don't know. Just suddenly feelin' my years, I guess."

"Why, you still got baby fat on your face, L. D.," she teased, edging around the coffee table and sitting beside him. "And anyway, you gave *me* a hard enough time when I turned thirty."

He grinned, straightening so he could slip his arm around her shoulders. "Yeah, s'pose I did. Anyhow, we're just spring chickens compared to a lot of people. Guess I'm just at that age when it finally sinks in that I'm never gonna do all the things in life I always thought I would."

She edged back just far enough to look into his eyes. "Aren't you happy with me, darlin'?"

"Aw, hell, I told you not to get your feelin's all hurt. Don't take things so dat-blamed personal all the time." He disengaged his arm from her and lowered his boots to the floor so he could sit up. Resting forearms on thighs, he stared down at the foam around the opening of his beer can and remembered the dreams that had driven him in his youth. Sarah must have read the sudden depression in his features, for she leaned forward to place a hand on his shoulder.

"What in the world's got you so blue, L. D.?" she asked with concern. "You were okay this morning. Something happen at work?"

He inhaled deeply and sucked on his teeth. "Well, yeah, it did." He continued to stare into his beer. "Charlie Lyles."

"*Cowboy* Lyles?" she asked.

"Cowboy, Roper, Charlie, what the hell's the difference. Fact remains, the sheriff's department over in Jim Ned County got in a warrant for his arrest yesterday. They tried servin' it at his mother's house over on Walnut Creek, but he wasn't there, so they passed it along to us."

"But I thought he was doing so well, L. D."

L. D. nodded. "He was a model prisoner down in Huntsville, kept his nose clean ever since he got out last January."

"So what's a warrant doing coming in that way, darlin'?"

L. D. guzzled the last of the beer and crushed the can in his hand. "He wasn't reportin' to his parole officer. I know it's the law, but ain't *that* a helluva reason for gettin' your parole revoked." He dropped the empty can into the wastebasket at his elbow. "He'll be like a wild mustang penned up this time—and that ain't no way for a cowboy to have to live."

Sarah ran caressing fingers along the back of his neck. "I know he's your best friend and all, L. D., but you can't go carrying all his burdens on yourself."

L. D. exhaled sharply. "If he's in Sims County, *I'm* the one's gotta arrest him. That's burden enough for anybody."

"How much more time will he have to serve out for stealing that jeep? Didn't he liked to have beat a man to death, too?"

L. D. nodded. "He served seven months out of four, so he's lookin' at a good three and a half years now."

Sarah took a deep breath and sat back, passing a hand over her forehead. "I just don't understand him, L. D., can't figure out why he keeps getting in trouble. And not reporting to his parole officer—it just don't make sense."

L. D. remembered a thousand days with Charlie, a thousand little details adding up to one reality. "It does if you're tryin' to cope where you don't belong, if you don't have any more business in the nineteen nineties than a good night horse or a lead steer on a cattle drive."

"Oh, L. D., don't make excuses for him," Sarah said impatiently. "There's just some people that can't stay out of trouble, just like there's some like you that make something out of themselves. Why, didn't you tell me that working that ranch y'all both used to say you'd been born a hundred years too late, that y'all should've lived back in the eighteen hundreds when there was a real place for cowboys and ever'thing?"

L. D. turned and stared into her eyes. "Yeah, but there's one difference—I think Charlie really believed it when *he* said it. And you know what? Deep inside all these years I've admired him for goin' ahead and tryin' to be the real cowboy he knows he oughta be, for not turnin' his back on his dreams. Hell, if *I've* had that kinda guts."

"Why, darlin', you're high sheriff of the whole county. Ever'body likes you and looks up to you. What else do you *want*?"

L. D. exhaled testily and stood to start for the kitchen and another beer. "Hell, I don't know—just to be able to look back when my life's all gone and be able to say, 'Hey, I did it; I had my dream and at least if I couldn't make it come true, it wasn't because I didn't try.'"

"Oh, L. D.," she said softly, watching him walk away, "you know you've just gotta keep your dreams from getting mixed up with what life really is."

He considered that thought all the way to the refrigerator, and he caught her eyes as soon as he reached the living room threshold again.

"That's just it," he said, lifting the tab with a pop. "Why do the two things have to be so different? Can't a man ever do what he thinks he ought to, be all the things he feels like he should?"

He eased in beside her again and drank long and deep, then became aware of her fingers soft on his neck. He glanced at her, catching the seductive smile, and set his beer on the coffee table. "Aw, hell, what am I talkin' about. Just sittin' here feelin' sorry for myself 'cause I thought I didn't have a damned thing better to do." He pulled her close and grinned. "I can think of *one* thing."

He heard that deep sigh of Sarah's that was almost a moan, and his mouth found hers, fierce and eager. And for long, passionate moments they sat curled in each other's arms, smooching and laughing like newlyweds.

A knock sounded on the front door. "Dat-gum it," L. D. said, glancing over. He could smell the freshness of her hair, feel it soft against the nape of his neck. "Tell 'em to go away."

"Oh, L. D.," she said, smiling as she disengaged herself. "Might be something important."

He watched the graceful, feminine swing of her hips as she crossed to the door. She opened it to a screech and a uniformed man with blue nylon windbreaker and black holster tipped his felt western hat. "Evening, Sarah. L. D. home? I sure need him right now."

"Why, hi, Milton," she said politely, pushing open the screen and motioning with her head. "Sure, he's right here."

The slender man of twenty-three with freckles jeweling his ruddy face stepped inside as the leather gun belt creaked. "Howdy, L. D.," he said, finding the older man on the sofa. "Sorry to bother you this way."

L. D. sighed and reached for his beer; he knew Milton looked upon him with almost hero worship, but damn it, couldn't he ever do anything for himself? "Hell, Milton, you ain't botherin' me. Here I got a cold beer and a pretty woman all to myself—can't imagine why I wouldn't be just tickled to death to see you." He stood, sipping from the can. "What's up?"

Milton Forster scratched the back of his head, tilting his hat forward as he did. "You're not gonna b'lieve this, L. D."

L. D. set his beer down and straightened, for he read the seriousness in his deputy's face. "Try me."

"The Walter McBee place, up on the Divide, that little shack about a mile off 2038. This don't make sense, but about sundown somebody just walked up there with a rifle and stole a horse from a wetback and just rode him off."

"They *what*?" exclaimed L. D.

"Damndest thing I ever heard of, L. D.," said the younger man, tugging at his belt. "McBee said the wet came driving up to the main ranch house and told him it was a big hombre, hadn't shaved in a while. Said he saddled up a bay gelding, grabbed a little food and water, a bunch of twenty-two shells and a carton of Camels, and lit out. Last time he saw him he was riding like hell right dead into the sunset."

L. D. glanced at his wristwatch. "That was an hour and half, hour and forty-five minutes ago. Call just come in?"

"Sure thing. Didn't know what to make of it, thought I better get you."

L. D. went to the closet by the lamp and came out wearing his Stetson and dangling a .357 magnum at the end of a gun belt.

"L. D.?" said Sarah with concern, watching him buckle it on. "I don't understand it, why somebody'd want to do something like that."

He looked straight into her eyes for just a moment. "Don't you?" he asked, and then he was headed for the door, his deputy a step ahead. When L. D. reached it, he looked back to find her brow ridged in confusion. He nodded. "He's done it, Sarah. Dat-blamed if somebody ain't finally had the guts to go and chase all those dreams that life never gives us for free."

And as he stepped out into the night air, he didn't know whether to feel heartened or heartsick.

L. D. knelt in the borrow ditch before the gate and ran his fingers over the crushed clump of grass illuminated by the headlights of the patrol car idling behind him. Moisture clung to his hand, courtesy of the dew which freshened the night air beyond the drifting exhaust fumes that wrinkled his nose. When he looked up, he saw his shadow stretched out against the small oak-and-mesquite mott brooding over a barbed-wire fence with cedar posts.

You don't like it any better than I do, do you, Charlie, he thought. *Fencin' up something that don't belong to nobody.*

"I'm tellin' you, that there boy went right through that gate."

An old man was talking and pointing as he loomed over L. D. He was seventy-five or so, by the quake in his voice and the sagging, leathery face.

"I tracked him just 'fore good dark, plumb from the little shack, clean up the lane to where he crossed the pavement. He followed that fence line all the way to the gate. Inside, if you look right close, you can see where he had that ol' horse in a gallop by the time he was three horse lengths inside it." He had a catch in his stride as he took a step nearer the fence to study the cedars and mesquites, wraith-like in the heavy shadows beyond. "What in the hell you think that boy's up to, anyhow?"

"Nobody but a crazy guy—or a drunk one—would do something like that," said Milton, patting his holster with the side of his fist. "Golly, L. D., what I wouldn't give to know what's going through his mind right now."

L. D. stood, and the dark beyond the gate seemed to reach out and flood him, just like he knew it did the rider. *You and me know plenty, don't we, Charlie.*

He glanced at the two men silhouetted against the stark brightness of the headlights. He nodded to the gate and fixed his eyes on the shadows that hid the trail. "Mr. McBee, can you tell me what's out there?"

The older man was taking a pinch of Scold. "Yeah, well, I'll tell you just like it is. I been ranchin' this country here ever since nineteen hundred and thirty-six, and my daddy started in aught-five. From here to those railroad tracks over the other side of Green Mountain—you know, by 156 there close to that country church—it's forty-seven miles as the crow flies. We're better'n twenty-five hundred feet right here, and when you start droppin' off in them canyons you ain't but nineteen or twenty. 'Twixt here and those tracks, and 'twixt the county seat on the east and that little town thirty-two miles to the west of it, you got your Divide country and your Colorado River watershed canyons. Expect there's a thousand or two sections of country with nothin' but a few ranch roads crossin' it. The flats up here on the Divide run out over that lower country like a bunch of bony and broke fingers. Up here where we are now we got some grassland that's pretty open except for a few scrubby cedars, some prickly pear, maybe some thorny shrubs and broomweeds. Even on top ever' dat-blamed thing either bites you or sticks you.

"You drop down in them canyons, though, and brother, I want to tell you, you're in for it. Steep and rocky, just a bunch of cliffs in a lot of places, and brush . . . talk about *brush*. Why, you danged sure better have your chaps on you're ridin' through *that* country. I guarantee you, you don't want to be found down in them canyons, you ain't gonna be."

L. D. shifted position so he could look at the older man without being blinded by the car lights. "Where's that wet at now?"

"Aw, back up at the main ranch house there. That fellow didn't hurt him none, but he's too shook up to stay out at that shack by hisself."

"I want to talk to him," said L. D. And, to the younger man, "Milton, you take the hand radio and the shotgun and park yourself here for a while, make sure that rider don't try to come back through here. Meantime, I'm gonna get the highway patrol out here to watch this road tonight, case he comes out another pasture. Prob'ly get the game wardens out too to cover 156 over by that little church—can't take a chance on him somehow gettin' all the way across that rough country tonight. Might better try and get some more manpower from Jim Ned County, that Department of Public Safety helicopter out of Midland. Anyway you figure it, looks like we got a manhunt on our hands."

L. D. again found the older man's face, one side flooded in light, the other shadowy. "Mr. McBee, you got a string of horses, good ridin' horses, don't you? You s'pose you could let us have some by daybreak tomorrow, some saddles? If that rider don't come out tonight, we gotta go in after him."

"Oblige you any way I can," said McBee. He spat, the sickly sweet odor of snuff catching the currents. "But can you boys tell me just who in the devil'd do somethin' like this?"

L. D. breathed deeply and turned his head to the gate, and again a thousand memories deluged him. "A cowboy—a damned good one," he said quietly.

The only response was the chirping of crickets from the brushy canyons hidden by the dark.

Chapter Three

A fence row immediately at Charlie's left herded him due
north through a grassy flat interspersed with low cedars and
biting shrubs. Overhead, buzzards were silhouetted against
a still-light sky, but the thickening vegetation ahead held
only creeping shadows. He kept the horse in a gallop until
the ground turned rocky a third of a mile from the highway,
then slowed to let the gelding gingerly pick its way through
prickly pear and thorny bushes.

The darkening brush squeezed close, the spidery, dead
limbs of cedars strafing Charlie's legs. He found himself on
the rim of a sharply etched canyon that gouged through the
bedrock to expose it in layers on the briary far wall. Through
the brush and shadows, the gorge looked to be as deep as a
hundred feet and as narrow as a few yards down in its cedar
brakes.

Ducking under the probing limbs of a dead cedar, he
urged the gelding to the edge of the first rock shelf. The
horse resisted, advancing only by constantly shifting its
forefeet as horseshoes clanged against stone. At the brink,
Charlie found a drop-off of several feet and only sharp-
pronged limbs below that. He backed the horse away until
he cleared the dead cedar, then he turned the animal eastward and began picking his way along the canyon rim.

It was getting dark. The red-streaked sky above was fading and the prickly pear and underbrush were increasingly

difficult to navigate. He had to make the canyon bottom, and if he didn't do it soon he wouldn't be able to. Nightfall would catch him here on the flats, a few hundred yards from the highway, and at daybreak the Divide might be swarming with searchers.

Thirty yards down-canyon he turned the horse through a break in the undergrowth to find a similar ledge, and did so twice more in the next forty yards. For once, he wished for a sure-footed mule. Finally, with dark closing in and visibility dropping, he decided to risk everything on the gelding's night vision and innate balance. He reined the animal through clawing limbs, felt it search for footing at the canyon brink, and, despite the horse's protests, forced it over the drop-off.

He immediately gave the gelding its head, letting it slip and slide down through the terraced rock and plow through the brush with a great cracking of limbs. He kept his toes' backed part-way out of the stirrups to avoid a hang-up were he forced to bail out of the saddle quickly. He could feel the gelding's heartbeat through his legs and sense its struggle to stay afoot, but finally they broke through a last line of shielding timber and gained the canyon floor.

Though cedars hovered on either side to render it murky, Charlie could tell by the metallic strike of the horseshoes that the drainage bed was of solid rock and strewn with stones. Barely wide enough for two horses abreast, it stretched generally west-east to die in the gloom, while higher up the silhouetted outline of timber defined the canyon rim.

Charlie had never been here before, but he knew this country. He knew that this canyon drained the Divide, any runoff it carried eventually emptying into the Colorado River or one of its tributaries. The Divide lay behind him and to the west. That meant the canyon dead-ended to his left, and soon, judging by how relatively shallow and narrow it was at this point. It was too dark to risk the opposite bluff, and anyway, knowing the lay of the land, he figured the flats to the north to be a neck of country waiting to fall off again into the breaks. At any rate, daybreak had to find him in the concealing undergrowth, so that left only down-canyon to travel.

First, though, he wanted to give them something to think about. He turned his horse to the west and went seventy-five or a hundred yards up the gorge, taking care to break a few limbs along the way. Then he reined the gelding about and headed down-canyon, a sneer parting his stubble.

Soon a hard dark fell over the land, the starry sky alone holding a faint glow. The brush came alive with a chorus of crickets, keeping time with the rhythmic hooves, and a shadow that was an owl came swooping up-canyon to veer into the timber and hoot. Something stirred against the bluff, rustling the undergrowth, and birds flitted about, disturbed from their roosts.

But Charlie, for the moment, felt a measure of peace. He was *back*, riding a wild country that welcomed him home though he had never been here before. The strange exaltation came over him again, for in this canyon unbridled by man time no longer existed; the decade could have been the eighteen nineties as easily as the nineteen nineties.

And there was again a place for a cowboy.

The canyon swung northward within a mile and widened little-by-little. Charlie could tell it deepened, too, by the uplift of the skyline that loomed at two hundred feet by the time he reached the confluence with an east-west drainage at about four miles. That meant another canyon, originating somewhere in the higher country to the west.

He passed it up just far enough to snap a twig or two, then reined his horse about and took it, the clock turning back further with every stride.

Within a few minutes he came to a water gap, multiple strands of twisted barbed wire forced several feet off the drainage bed by a gnarled timber carried by past runoff.

Cursing the fence, as he always did, he derived grim pleasure in snapping the lower strand with the wire cutters to let his horse pass. Still, though he removed his hat and hugged the saddle horn to avoid the higher strands, a barb caught him in the shoulder.

The canyon walls gradually squeezed in as the gorge veered southwest, and two miles beyond the water gap he took yet another drainage, this one off to his right. He followed it for a couple of hundred yards before it steepened dramatically. Dismounting, he unsaddled the horse and staked it at the length of the catch-rope to allow the animal to graze the sparse grass. Then, sagging tiredly to the rocky ground under an overhanging cedar, he lay back against the saddle and lit a long-anticipated cigarette.

And with every draw, the memories came back.

He was astride a horse, a diminutive rider of seven amid the boiling dust of a warped wooden pen seething with milling and bellowing cattle. Nearby, two boots were propped side-by-side on the bottom fence rail; one belonged to the ranch foreman, the other to a new hand. Neither man stirred at the sharp stench of hair and flesh sizzling before an orange-hot branding iron. But the newcomer did straighten at the sight of Charlie's catch-rope darting out from his cutting horse like the strike of a rattler.

"Whose kid is he?" asked the new hand.

"Nobody's here. Lives over close to Greenleaf, few miles away. Name's Charlie. We call him Roper or Cowboy. Ain't got no daddy. They say his mama ain't nothin' but a drunk and a whore."

"How come he ain't in school? That boy can't be over seven years old."

"Can't keep him there. They say he keeps sneakin' out, winds up out here or some other ranch, always foolin' with the horses. Say he's been doin' that ever since he was five. They'll come drag him back in to school ever so often, kickin' and screamin' bloody murder. Hell, used to carry

him back myself for a while, 'fraid he was gonna git hurt. I fin'lly got to where I don't pay no attention to him—I ain't never seen nobody so born to the saddle. Damned if he ain't a better hand right now than any of these wetbacks."

"Boy that age needs to be in school," opined the new hand, unconvinced. "What's his mother think?"

"Hell, she don't care. Never has. *This cow camp's got to where it's about the only home he knows—spends more time out here than he does in his own bed."*

As he took one last drag on the cigarette and sank to find sleep twenty-five years later, Charlie's bed was the rocky floor of a hidden canyon and his pillow a well-worn saddle.

Thursday, June 3

By daybreak when L. D. reached for the reins of the gelding tied to the back of the horse trailer in the borrow ditch, the other members of the party already were mounted: Milton on a roan, old man McBee on an appaloosa, Texas Ranger captain Gene Syers and another ranger on bays, and Jim Ned County Sheriff Ernest Fowler and a deputy on brown horses. All except McBee sported an obvious rifle, shotgun, or pistol, and L. D. didn't question the elderly man about the bulge that meant a six-shooter tucked in his shirt. After all, at seventy-five he had volunteered to track an armed fugitive across his ranch—an offer L. D. would have refused in a second had he not realized McBee knew the land better than anybody, even Charlie. Besides, he thought, the old man was the only one who looked as if he had ever spent more than a day on a horse. The others, despite their professed horsemanship and western hats, looked uncomfortable as the devil.

Reins in hand, L. D. reached for the saddle horn and planted a boot in the left stirrup. The sudden weight on one side of the saddle brought the horse wheeling. L. D. knew what that meant—a fresh horse, pastured for months—but it was too late to do anything about it. Downing its head, the gelding began to pitch, sending L. D. sprawling to the grassy borrow ditch.

As the horse went bucking across the pavement, caustic laughter sounded. L. D. looked up past the breast of a bay horse to see Gene Syers' derisive smile. "Hell of a cowboy *you* must've been, Hankins. See if you can't keep your butt on him next time—we're wasting precious minutes waiting on you."

Damn, thought L. D., disgusted at himself and feeling every bit as overweight as he was. But as he readjusted his leggings and crawled back to his feet with the help of the trailer fender, it wasn't frustration that reddened his face; it was his dislike of the Texas Ranger with the flat, crooked nose and scar tissue above his hardened eyes—souvenirs of some long-ago barroom fight, L. D. had been told. He had never respected Syers as a person, only as a law enforcement officer; he'd always considered the fifty-year-old with the big-city ways too hard-nosed, too much by-the-book. He was a cynical, arrogant bastard.

Milton came leading the horse back across the highway, and as L. D. reached for the reins again, McBee nodded to the animal. "Better cheek him this time, son—you know, bring his head 'round to his shoulder."

"Yes, sir," said L. D. politely, inwardly resenting that someone thought he had to be told that. Hell, he and Charlie had spent three years with the JAs off the caprock in that Big Red country near Amarillo, twenty-eight months of it in a line camp.

But as he mounted, he realized this marked the first time in eight years he had been on a horse. He seemed to fill up a lot more of the saddle now, and his belly slipped over his belt to nudge the horn. He just hoped he could hold up the way he used to on those thirty-mile rides through the breaks on the JAs.

But even as he followed McBee through the gate as dawn streaked the sky red over the east-side greenery, his joints were stiff and his eyes tired. He had been up most of the night, talking with the Mexican hand, requesting the assistance of other law enforcement agencies, studying maps, coordinating the search. And while the six men with him made up the largest party, he had dispatched several other groups of two to four officers each to man roadblocks along highways 2038 and 156, check abandoned shacks in the canyons, inquire at area ranches. Too, the receding highway held the bubble and rotors of a DPS helicopter, its pilot and trooper-passenger readying to scour the cedar brakes. It was an effort comprising four agencies—the sheriff's departments of Sims and Jim Ned counties, Department of Public Safety, and Parks and Wildlife Department—and involving more than a score officers, including four Texas Rangers.

A lone cowboy on a stolen horse had brought on the biggest stir L. D. had ever seen in this county of two thousand people, and deep inside he felt a dark depression at instigating it. He was betraying Charlie—or was he? Maybe it was Charlie who had betrayed him, by putting him in the position of having to choose between duty and friendship.

"Say, Hankins." Syers' raspy voice brought L. D. glancing over his shoulder at the trailing horses nodding along in a slow gait. "What the hell makes you think it's this Lyles we're after?"

L. D. took in the alert eyes of Jim Ned County Sheriff Ernest Fowler, a rangy, hawk-faced man riding beside Syers. "You know him, Ernest. Least, you've had dealin's with him."

Fowler cupped his hands to his face in lighting a cigarette and nodded.

"For one thing," L. D. went on, "the physical description fits him: big man, early thirties, boots split down the front. And what he's doin' fits him."

"That boy always said he was born a hundred years too late," spoke up McBee, leaning over and studying the rider's trail.

Syers laughed lowly. "Still playing cowboys and Indians, is he? Bet he's wishing he hadn't, once he sobered up this morning. Especially if he's got any idea there's a ranger or two on his tail. We'll have this drugstore cowboy rounded up in time to go have us a steak over in the county seat, make time with the waitress. You seen that redhead they got working there? Anyway, wouldn't surprise me any if he didn't come riding back in on his own—anybody out in this rough a country'll be looking for the door out damned quick."

L. D.'s face flushed hot at the man's arrogance. "Not if you're Charlie Lyles, you won't."

Syers swept an arm in front of him derisively. "Hell, he's nothing but a two-bit punk joy-riding. Just took a horse instead of a car, that's all. I've seen his kind clear from Houston to El Paso."

L. D. straightened in the saddle. "You ain't *never* seen nobody like Lyles," he snapped, his agitation evident.

Milton Forster brought his horse up alongside L. D.'s. "Why *did* he take that horse, L. D.? There was a pickup sitting right there."

L. D. nodded to the green brush and undergrowth ahead. "Look where you're ridin', Milton. Try takin' a pickup through *this.*"

"But he could have been in Mexico by now, drinking tequila in some joint," said the young deputy.

L. D. leaned over in the saddle, tracing the hoofprints with a lowered arm. "Yeah—providin' it was the law he was tryin' to get away from in the first place."

"SOB's got a prison sentence hanging over him," snarled Syers. "What the hell else would he be trying to get away from?"

L. D. sat back up and stared straight into a horizon without concrete or steel or asphalt. "The nineteen nineties."

Syers spat a stream of tobacco juice down by his bay's front hoof. "Hell, you're as crazy as he is. I'll tell you *one* thing—if he *is* loony enough to go playing cowboys and

Indians out here, he's liable to pretend we're the Indians and go to raising that rifle of his." He patted the semi-automatic Ruger .223 he held crossways on his thighs. "This thing'll cut that SOB in half."

L. D. again fixed his eyes on the uplifted turf marking the trail of the night before, but his mind was with the rider at its end. *Don't lift it, Charlie*, he pleaded silently.

The tracks were plain enough alongside the south-to-north fence, but upon veering away at the thickening brush, they dimmed in the rocky ground.

"Where the hell did he go?" Syers asked, impatiently scouring the brush.

But L. D. and McBee were too busy studying the rocks chipped bone-white by the strike of iron shoe to answer. L. D. had never tracked anyone before, but he knew enough about horses to recognize the obvious signs of one's passage: the chips, the dirt-side-up pebbles, the upturned rocks, the crushed filaree growing up through a crack, the fresh break in a tender young limb. What worried L. D. was that Charlie *knew* he'd be able to identify all these things. What would the cowboy do to try to shake them?

"That dead cedar—see it, son?"

McBee was stationary, pointing, talking. "He went right up to the edge of that canyon there." He started to prod his horse forward, but L. D.'s outstretched arm stilled him.

"Better let us check it, Mr. McBee. Don't know what's down there."

Dismounting, he handed the reins to the elder man and edged around the cedar's finger-like limbs. He was conscious for the first time of the .357 magnum rubbing his hip, and a deep breath passed his lungs. *Don't be there, Charlie. I know you'd never hurt me, never hurt anybody unless you was hemmed up like a wild mustang that just wanted to live the only way it can.*

Which was exactly what Charlie was right now.

As soon as L. D. hung the toes of his boots over the

drop-off to see the brush below, he knew the horseman hadn't come this way. Retreating, he shook his head to McBee and mounted to ride eastward along the rim.

Identifying three other places down-canyon where the brushy precipice had turned the rider away, they finally came upon telltale marks. Here, iron-shod hooves had clipped the rock on the way down—and the severity of the slope told L. D. reams about the degree of Charlie's desperation.

"I know how hard it is to cross that canyon," allowed McBee, squinting his crow's-footed eyes to study the gorge from the saddle. "You need a devil of a good horse and daylight to do it in."

"Charlie didn't *have* daylight," said L. D., folding his hands over the saddle horn.

"Hell, *we* do," snapped Syers, unable to see from his angle the trail of chipped ledges, upturned rocks, and broken limbs. "What's the holdup? Let's stay on that SOB's butt."

L. D. read the danger and looked around at Syers. "I don't know—that's pretty tough, looks to me. Maybe we better—" The clang of iron against rock brought L. D. turning just in time to see McBee force his gelding off the shelf.

"Looka there!" Syers exclaimed smugly. "That old man's not afraid of a little hill!" And then to the Jim Ned deputy astride the brown horse in front of him, "Hey, deputy—get that horse down there before somebody shoots that old coot."

L. D. started to stretch out a hand and hold the man's horse up, but he'd had enough conflict with Syers already and didn't want to aggravate matters. So he backed his mount away from the rim a few feet and watched the deputy nudge the reluctant horse up to the ledge and off.

L. D. knew the man was in trouble the moment he went over, for he kept a tight rein, refusing the horse its instinctive actions.

"Give him his head!" he yelled.

Sparks flew as horseshoes struck stone. The rider's hat tumbled as he fell across the saddle horn. With its burden suddenly shifting, the horse stumbled in the angling scree between terraces. A hoof plowed through dirt and caught hard against upraised bedrock, collapsing the foreleg. To sudden, frenzied neighing and the rider's cry, the gelding went down hard to its breast and then to its side, eight hundred pounds of animal crushing the deputy's leg as it rolled with him. Throwing him free as it fell away, the horse thundered head-over-hooves through a storm of dust all the way down the bluff, caving off sections of ledge, uprooting rocks, bowling over trees to a fierce snapping of limbs.

A hundred feet below on the canyon floor, it came to rest—carrion for the circling buzzards.

Chapter Four

The rocky ground was hard and uneven and the gelding restless, yet Charlie slept better than he had in a long while. He wasn't prone to philosophical reflections—few cowboys were. All he knew was that here lay the indefinable something he needed and craved, a quality or quantity without which his life would remain as empty and lonely as a cattle trail with no stock.

He awoke while darkness still blanketed the canyon and cut open a can of pork and beans with his pocketknife. The night had cooled to the point that grease had congealed on top, but he sopped it up hungrily with stale bread. The crickets chirped musically while he ate, and afterward, while he smoked, the rustle of an armadillo in the undergrowth brought his head turning.

They'll be comin' in this mornin', he thought, *chasin' a cowboy on a rode-down horse, but they won't be catchin' up to either one. Maybe yesterday, maybe when it was the nineteen nineties, but not now, not here, not no more.*

Then he stood, casting his eyes back in the direction of the pasture gate, and concern furrowed his face as the hoarse words came in a whisper. "Don't come after me, L. D. Ain't you or nobody takin' me back, not to the nineteen nineties or that jail cell or anywhere else 'cept right here where I belong."

Thumping the glowing butt to the drainage bed, he threw the blanket across the gelding's withers and saddled up.

A cool east breeze pushed at Charlie's back as the horse picked its way up the abrupt grade marking the canyon head. Frequently, low-lying limbs forced him to bend one way or another, and the thick underbrush tangled with thorny briars made him wish for his leggings. Throughout, shod hooves grated against rock. Twice the horse veered to avoid stone terraces, then gained the next level through chutes unseen to Charlie. Finally, two hundred feet above the canyon floor, the gelding topped out.

Charlie stopped, placing a hand on the cantle of his saddle and twisting around to the squeak of leather. Solitary buttes and jutting fists of the Divide stood against a red sky as dawn crept almost imperceptibly across the breaks. Cool currents fresh with cedar stayed in his face as he scanned the horizon, his eyes stopping on the windmill skylined on timbered tableland less than a mile to the northeast.

Charlie didn't need water. At every stride of the bay, the jug bound to the saddle horn sloshed with almost a gallon. But he wasn't the only one to consider. He turned back in the saddle, feeling the gelding's restlessness. He knew that a horse, when given the opportunity, normally would water two or three times a day in hot weather—and he also knew how important the animal was to him right now, in more ways than he could count.

But pickup roads traced these finger-like peninsulas jutting out over the breaks; how long could he risk the relative exposure of the Divide when oncoming daylight would demand he cross this narrow neck and fall back into the canyons?

With full dawn still several minutes away, he loped the gelding for the mill through rocks and cedars that gave way to a park-like grassland dotted with shrubs and prickly pear. A deer went bounding across their path on spring-loaded legs, its tail a white flag waving in the shadows. Another minute and he burst upon several dark forms bedded on the flat. They were white-faced cattle, stirring at the staccato of the horse's easy gait. Then one exploded to its hooves and they all did, surging away as a single frenzied mass amid thunder and dust. It constituted a stampede, in its own small way, and it set Charlie's mind reeling with images of line shacks, roping pens, and tack houses where stove-up old cowboys rolled smokes and looked squint-eyed down at a young admirer eager to devour their every word. With voices choked by old alkali dust but still alive with profanity, they told him of honest-to-goodness stampedes on one-day cattle drives to the railroad or thirty-day pushes through seldom-fenced country to Horsehead Crossing on the Pecos and ranches beyond. And sometimes the voices trailed away and the leathery faces, etched and hardened by a lifetime under the sun, sagged just a little, as the old-timers realized again that their day had passed.

It had been plenty rough back then before mechanization, Charlie thought, driving wild steers through wilder country, riding from daybreak to dark with nothing to look forward to each night but a lumpy bedroll and a two-hour guard shift. On clear days the dust had crawled down a man's throat until he couldn't breathe, and on stormy ones a thunderstorm perhaps had charged the air until the electricity clung to his spurs. Maybe his horse had ended up finding a prairie dog hole, or an angry longhorn his ribs; men had died, but at a dollar a day none of them had died rich. Yet, for a cowboy who knew no other way to live, maybe it had been better.

With that thought came other images, chief among them a nameless man lashing out at him with switch or belt or just sheer hands. There were many such men, but they all blurred into one scowling face reeking with whiskey, while the features of their lady-friend always remained distinct. A haggard woman with stringy dark hair and the puffy and lined face of an alcoholic, she stood uncaring and thick-tongued at the side, urging her current live-in suitor to beat the hell out of the little troublemaker.

Within a thousand yards the brush thickened, and Charlie pulled up to look through a dead cedar and find a gaping canyon, a quarter-mile wide, separating him from the windmill. He couldn't trace the near rim for the timber at his face, but he could make out the far terraced rock pushing northwestward as the canyon gouged into the tableland. There, several hundred yards away, it headed at a rock pour-off stained with minerals.

Day continued to break; the overhead sky now held streaks of red extending from the horizon. Charlie hadn't counted on a gulch blocking his route; if he had, he would have crossed this neck of land in the pre-dawn shadows and hoped for a mill or dirt tank down in the breaks beyond. His reaction now was to turn his horse into the concealing brush rimming the gorge and make for the pour-off marking its head.

He delayed a decision on whether to seek out the windmill, or to push on across the flat to the unseen breaks, until he reached the ravine head and checked the dawning sky. He found sunrise imminent and the timber a hindrance, but he figured if he veered into the exposed flats and rode hard for the sentineling tower to the east-southeast, he would go unnoticed a few minutes more.

Besides, the horse was just as outcast in the nineteen nineties as Charlie, and he damned sure wasn't going to mistreat it the way he had been.

He struck an eroded ranch road in obvious disuse and took the horse down the ruts straight for the windmill and sunrise. Exposed, driven, and pressed for time, he suddenly twitched at a growing sound that sharply contrasted with the drumming of hooves and whistling of a redbird. It was like the rapid beating of many wings, a choppy whir and mechanical whine that should not have been here in the past where Charlie rode.

He could tell by the way the animal pointed its ears that something had seized its attention low over the greenery fringing the canyon system to the south. Charlie looked, too, catching the glint of first sunlight from something rising over the scrub oaks and stunted cedars. The object veered a few degrees, negating the glare, and Charlie saw the bubble of a helicopter bearing down on him from almost straight ahead. It came swooping upon him so abruptly that all he could do was rein his horse strongly into a chittam mott at the left and fight to keep the animal's head up in response to the quick tightening of its shoulder muscles. Still, the gelding swerved at the shrill drone of rotors and grated Charlie's thigh against a tall, straight bole. He looked up through umbrella-like foliage at the craft passing overhead and a gale-force downdraft wrenched the limbs. A storm of twigs and leaves stung his face, and in reflexively ducking he relaxed the reins and the animal downed its head and began pitching wildly.

Caught off-balance, Charlie weathered the jumps until a sinewy trunk seized his shoulder and peeled him backwards from the saddle. The rifle went flying but a cowboy's instinct made him hold doggedly to the reins with one hand.

The sky spun crazily through the greenery and his temple scraped rough bark, then he came down hard on his collar bone to find flailing hooves at his eyes. He was stunned, but not so much so that he didn't immediately lunge for and seize the reins with his free hand. He stubbornly refused to let go even as the spooked gelding dragged him through the underbrush; being set afoot in a pasture was bad enough anytime, but this was a situation desperate beyond measure.

After a few feet the horse calmed and came to a standstill—but Charlie did not. Searching the sky criss-crossed by limbs for the helicopter, he reached for the rifle to brandish it angrily at the sudden intrusion of the nineteen nineties into a cowboy's world.

The radio at L. D.'s saddle crackled, but he was afoot and stumbling down the slope with the clumsiness of one who had let himself grow soft. He was huffing like a chased-down steer by the time he reached the injured man, who lay groaning and writhing at the brink of a drop-off, his face wrenched and his hands clutching a shin that oozed blood. L. D. had seen a lot of men thrown and a few get hurt seriously, and he knew as soon as he knelt at the bloody jag of bone protruding through jeans that this wasn't a fall from which a rider would get up and walk away.

Crying out the deputy's name, Fowler came down at L. D.'s heels. Milton, too, dismounted to rush toward the rim, but as he brushed past L. D.'s horse, the radio crackled again and he turned and seized it.

"You hurt bad, Ed?" cried Fowler, bending over his deputy. "Ed, you hurt bad?"

Bad, thought L. D., watching the blood smear the ledge to the death-like throes, *plenty bad*.

He dug a knee into the rock at the edge of the drop-off to keep the man from rolling over. "We gotta watch out for shock," he said, sliding a hand under the deputy's head. He glanced at the horse at the canyon bottom and then looked past Fowler's pale features at Milton framed against a twisted cedar on the rim. "Milton! Get down there and pull that blanket off that horse! We gotta cover him up! He's liable to go into shock!"

"It's the chopper, L. D.! They've sighted something close to a windmill a few miles over! Just got a glimpse—could be him! They want to set down and check it out!"

Even as L. D. looked back at the injured man's twisted features and all the blood at his leg, a quick thought passed through his mind: *Damn it, Charlie, how could you have been so careless?* Then he spun again to the young deputy.

"Call 'em off! Get that helicopter over here! We got a man hurt bad!"

"But L. D., they've—"

"Tell 'em to get the ground support team over there—if there's a windmill there's gotta be roads! And get that blanket damned quick!"

Within a few minutes the helicopter whirred by over-head, spooking the horses, and set down in the flats as close to the canyon as the timber allowed. L. D., Fowler, and Milton were still hovering over the injured man, keeping him as comfortable as possible, when the Texas Ranger named Powers came running back through the brush with the pilot and trooper. They found Syers still astride his bay at the rim, his hands folded across the saddle horn and callous indifference masking his face as he looked upon the scene below.

"How bad's he hurt?" blurted the trooper who wore the gray uniform and felt western hat of the Department of Public Safety.

Syers looked around, his eyes suddenly attentive. "Fell off his damned horse. What about that call? You see something or not?"

"Sure thought we did, heading off into a clump of trees up on top. If we could've set down we'd've had him, if that's who it was."

Syers exhaled in disgust and leaned over the opposite side of his saddle and spat. Meanwhile, the pilot had edged to the rim to make eye contact with L. D. and shake his head.

"No way I can carry him, Sheriff—that man needs to lay down, the back end of a pickup," he called out. "I'll go back and get hold of somebody. If it's all right to move him, go ahead and bring him on over to where I'm set down."

Syers shook his head firmly. "I want you men back up in the air," he said testily, sweeping his hand in the direction of the flats. "We'll make that call"—and with a glance down the slope and sarcasm in his voice—"won't we, *Sheriff.* Meantime, you men get over to that windmill, see what's there. I want that SOB caught by dinner time."

L. D., in glaring at Syers above, felt Milton's eyes suddenly on him, studying and questioning. He knew his young deputy expected him to spar with Syers at the ranger's wrenching of his authority, but with a man bleeding at their feet this wasn't the time. He turned to Milton and nodded to the radio in his hand. "Make it," he said.

Powers joined L. D. and the other two men in carrying the injured deputy up the slope. L. D., breathing harder than ever, hung his toe on the lip of the bluff and stumbled, putting the first scuff mark on his boot. He had just righted himself when, in brushing past Syers' bay, he felt the ranger take his upper arm. "I want to talk to you, Hankins," Syers said gruffly.

Now that they had the man up in the cedars, four persons were more a hindrance than an asset, bringing Milton to turn his head to L. D. "Go ahead, L. D.; we got him from here."

His eyes already riveted on Syers, L. D. stopped, allowing the injured deputy to slide through his relaxed fingers and into the others' care.

"Yeah?" he asked Syers, bracing for a confrontation.

"What the hell kind of stunt you pulling, calling that chopper over here?" demanded the ranger, enjoying the sense of dominance afforded by his vantage point on the horse. "They damned near had that SOB—and that thing wasn't a bit of good anyway in hauling a hurt man out of here."

L. D. slung a hand toward the canyon bottom, where McBee stood inspecting the dead horse. "We almost had a man killed—*you* almost had a man killed," he snapped. "A slope like that, we shoulda walked down, led the horses. All I knew was we had a man hurt bad and he needed help the fastest way we could get it. Anyway, *I* heard what they said—they didn't have any idea what they saw over there. Could've been anything, a cow or a deer or, yeah, maybe even Charlie. Whatever it was, it's still there and we can find it again."

Syers' cynical eyes narrowed as he stared down at L. D. "*Charlie*, is it? Just how well you know this Lyles, anyway?"

L. D. straightened, feeling a little intimidated at having to look up at a man who challenged him so. "Enough to know there ain't a one of us—you included—that's near the kind

of rider he is, that's half as much at home out here. He's a
cowboy like nobody else there is."

Syers studied him with penetrating eyes. "Sounds like
you kind of like that idea: some dumb old cowboy leading
us on a wild goose chase out here, making us all look bad."

L. D. flushed angrily. "Who got up this manhunt, anyway?" He flung a hand toward the broken ledge halfway
down the bluff. "And if you were so damned sure the helicopter was such a bad idea, why in the hell didn't you say
somethin' about it when I first called for it? Lyles is out
there somewhere, all right, but we can't sacrifice safety and
common-sense—like you tellin' that deputy to go on down
that slope—just to catch up to a cowboy."

"Cowboy, hell, he's a thief and convicted felon. I don't
know what your personal stake is in all this, Hankins, but
maybe you better back off a minute and make sure you
remember that."

The words followed Milton into the brush as he backed
along, supporting the injured man's shoulders, and he lifted
his eyes to look down the blood-soaked leg and find frowns
as deep as his own in the faces of Fowler and Powers.

"How'd the sheriff know this Lyles, anyway?" asked
Fowler.

Milton stiffened defensively. "They were friends; I think
they cowboyed together—but don't make anything out of
it. L. D. knows how to keep his personal feelings out of his
sheriffing, I guarantee you. They don't come any better than
L. D."

But as Milton twisted his head to guide his next step, the
rays at his eyes bespoke an ever-so-slight trace of confusion
and doubt.

Chapter Five

In the canyon bottom at midday, L. D. rode in silence, staring at the sweat foaming white between the hindquarters of the leading appaloosa. In spite of himself, he couldn't keep from mentally replaying the ugly scene with Syers, and what bothered him most was that, damn it, maybe the SOB was right. Maybe he *was* too emotionally involved in this whole episode; maybe he really *had* called for that chopper more to ensure the getaway of the blur in the brush than to aid the injured deputy. Maybe down deep he didn't even really want to catch Charlie. Hell, he didn't know.

When he'd taken this job he'd promised to do his damndest to make Sims County a better place to live, and he'd really meant it. But what did catching up to a rode-down cowboy have to do with it? The hell with parole violations and stolen horses! He knew that in Charlie's mind, you couldn't ever really *steal* something that nobody but a cowboy could lay claim to in the first place. A horse was a part of a cowboy's world, a part of Charlie's, and to separate the two was as big an injustice as forcing an Old West man to live in a New West world.

But here in this canyon land, the nineteen nineties and the men of its time were the intruders, and L. D. saw at every turn the difference between a would-be cowboy such as himself and the honest-to-God thing in Charlie. Already L. D.'s knees ached from supporting his weight in the stirrups; he'd never had this much lard to pack around alongside Charlie back on the JAs. Too, he'd forgotten what the bouncing gait of a horse in rough country did to the crotch; he wished for a jock strap, or at least something besides those baggy drawers Sarah kept getting him. Further, he never remembered the sharp, stabbing pains on the insides of his thighs at every stride, or his palm and fingers getting so red and sore from gripping the saddle horn in downgrades.

Not only all that, but when he studied the other riders the contrast between bogus and genuine was as pronounced as a gas station chamois up alongside stout saddle leather. McBee, on the leading appaloosa, evidently had been a competent horseman in his day, but now his seventy-five years were telling on him and his shoulders drooped as he sagged in the saddle. L. D. worried about him in this heat, for even though cedars twisted down from twenty-five feet to join oaks and red-berried shrubs in shading the canyon floor, the air already seemed to boil and the gusting wind was a branding fire in their faces.

The roan behind L. D., meanwhile, nodded along tenderfoot-style in the wake of the other horses, going when they went and stopping when they stopped; Milton, astride it, hadn't caught on yet to controlling it with the reins and pressure from his thighs. Powers, on the other hand, clutched the saddle horn at every stride as if he expected his bay to "break in two"—pitch wildly—at any second. Fowler, behind him, already winced with every bounce and often leaned forward in the saddle to rub his raw thighs.

Syers, on the trailing bay with the white band ringing one leg, caught L. D.'s backward glance and straightened in the saddle. He rode like a greenhorn, carrying too much weight on his thighs instead of his legs, but he alone was too stubborn to show the effects in his face. And when L. D. turned back around to watch McBee's appaloosa negotiate the drainage chute of solid rock curving through the brakes, it was the image of Syers' .223 Ruger glinting in brief sunlight that stayed strongest in his mind.

L. D. looked up past the prickly pear, growing out of boulders massing at his shoulder, to the oaks and elms higher on the slope; their limbs quaked in shades of green against a blue sky with white wisps. *You're out there somewhere, Charlie,* he thought, *not hurtin' nobody and not askin' any more than just to be left alone. But you know I'm comin' after you. You know I've got to.*

But the cowboy was making it tough on them. By mid morning they already had lost his trail twicc for long minutes, and after ducking under the freshly snipped wire at the uplifted water gap, they had followed this canyon an hour before its unassailable head turned them back. And now, as McBee stopped to lean over and point at the crisp, brown leaves blanketing the confluence with a lesser drainage to the left, L. D. didn't know whether to feel encouragement or regret.

"There," said the old man, spitting a stream of tobacco juice where he pointed. "See them leaves, how they's all mashed?" He lifted his head to the side canyon. "Right up there's where he went, I'll bet you all the way to the top."

"How many hours behind you think we are, L. D.?" asked Milton.

L. D. took off his hat and wiped his sweaty forehead. "Probably came through here last night sometime. Reckon he—"

"The hell with all this gabbing—it's too damned hot," interrupted Syers, brushing his bay past the stationary animals to come even with L. D. "You planning on getting this SOB or not?"

L. D. flushed. "You can't go chargin' hell with a water bucket—you've got to be careful, know what you're gettin' in to, just like this mornin' when that deputy—"

"If all you amateurs just stay out of my way I'll bring that cowboy in," snapped Syers, urging his gelding into the side canyon. He half-lifted the .223. "That bastard gives *me* any reason to use this thing, he better get those boots off damned quick if he don't want to die with 'em on."

"Hold on there a minute, Gene," spoke up Sheriff Fowler. "I don't know how bad everybody else in this bunch wants to catch Lyles, but I'm one of the ones that does."

"You implyin' somethin', Ernest?" asked L. D., suddenly feeling defensive.

Fowler didn't even give L. D. a glance. Instead, he nodded back to the south and then made eye contact with Syers, who had held his horse up and turned in the saddle. "That's a good boy that got hurt back there 'cause of him," Fowler continued, "a good boy from a nice family. But this is not the first time I've chased Lyles, and I don't know that we have to be in all that big a hurry. He's got a history of flubbing up, doing something stupid somewhere along the line and making it easy to catch him. Let's get off a minute, stretch our legs, let me tell you about it. Anyway, my back side's killing me."

The ranger captain grumbled a little, but he nevertheless dismounted, somewhat gingerly, along with the rest. Holding the reins of their horses, they stood working their joints and massaging sore knees or hips. L. D. found his own legs as stiff as firewood and his thighs tender, and sweat darkened his shirt where his belly hung over his belt. He already felt as if he'd just finished an all-day roundup in the breaks back on the JAs, and for the first time he wished that Sarah hadn't fed him all those damned desserts over the years.

"Y'all knew that Lyles got sent up to the pen at Huntsville," said Fowler, sliding a hand up the inside of his thigh. "Well, I'm the one that put him there, back when I was chief deputy, Jim Ned County. He stole an open-topped jeep from the Roy Johnson ranch over by Tinnie. We were out patrolling that area, got the call real quick, sighted him on a backcountry caliche road. We took in after him, lights a-flashing, and when he saw he couldn't outrun us he tried to get away by plowing that jeep right through a barbed wire fence." He paused to chuckle quietly. "That top strand peeled him right off."

Everyone snickered except L. D.—even Milton, until he saw his mentor's stoicism.

"Give the poor dumb SOB enough rope and he'll hang himself again," stated Fowler.

"That was there, not here," snapped L. D. "That was where there was cars and jeeps and all those things a real cowboy never knew nothin' about. That was in *your* world, Ernest, not Charlie's. Now he's got you in his—and jeeps are a damned sight scarce."

Only now did Fowler look at L. D. "Why is it you keep defending Lyles that way? I—"

"L. D.'s the best thing that ever happened to this county," spoke up Milton.

L. D. exhaled sharply. "Damn it, Milton, I can take up for myself," he chastised, catching the younger man's eyes. "*Let* him have his say." He turned back to Fowler and stared into his features. "Go ahead—let's get it all out in the open, once and for all."

Fowler took a deep breath and studied his eyes. "I thought I knew you pretty well, L. D., all that dove hunting we did together. I know you're a better law officer than to side with somebody that don't care any more about the man that gave him a job than to beat him up and steal a jeep from him."

L. D. straightened. "You want to know why he took that thing, Ernest, what brought on all the trouble? Yeah, the law says he stole that jeep and gave Johnson a good goin' over— I'll grant you that—but I'm not so sure I wouldn't've done the same damned thing if I'd've been in his boots."

Suddenly, all eyes were on L. D.

"I'm listening," said Fowler, unconvinced. "But you're not going to tell me anything I don't already know."

"Then I guess you know all about how Johnson used to spur his horses in the shoulders, cut 'em all up."

"I heard he was a little rough on them, all right," Fowler admitted.

"Well, did you ever hear about what he did to that horse that throwed him so hard way out in the pasture and left him on foot? He came back in the jeep with his catch-rope, tied him on the back end, led him back up toward the house so fast the horse stumbled and went down. He drug that horse till the rope broke, just ruined him, and when Charlie found out about it, he made damned sure it never happened again."

"And what in the hell gave *him* the right to tell a man how to treat his own horses?" snarled Syers. "If a man pays for something out of his own pocket he's got a right to do what he damned well pleases."

L. D. looked over at Syers and laughed lowly in disgust. "Somehow, I'm not surprised to hear that comin' from you, Syers. How 'bout you, Ernest? That how you feel?"

The Jim Ned County sheriff looked down and raked his boot through the leaves. "You can't go comparing an animal to a man, L. D. No matter what Johnson did to that horse, Lyles still didn't have the right to assault him and take that jeep—and you know it well as I do."

L. D. gave a caustic half-laugh. "I reckon Charlie and me both have seen a lot of men we wouldn't trade-even for a horse—and Johnson's one of 'em."

"I'll tell you what I *would* trade," spoke up the ranger named Powers, a gangly man of forty with shades and closely cropped brown hair. "I'd give my whole week's pay to have all this over with so I could be back home with the new baby, check on my wife."

L. D. was not sorry the topic of conversation had changed. "Y'all's first?" he asked.

Powers nodded, pride and a smile masking his face. "A boy, eight pounds, twelve ounces. This is my first day back on the job—not shaping up quite the way I planned it. Looks like this could be a long, drawed-out affair, doggone it."

"Enough of this baby talk," Syers said impatiently, hiding

his eyes behind military-style sunglasses and planting his boot in a stirrup. "Let's ride—and be damned quick about it."

Charlie was plunging his horse down the rocky escarpment marking the far side of the finger of land before he again heard the drone of the helicopter from somewhere behind. He looked ahead and down at the shadows of vultures gliding across the greenery of a broad canyon four hundred feet deep. Half a mile away he could see a fortification of stacked rock rimming a long, south-facing bluff, with timber in stark contrast to a bare swell far up-canyon to his left. Then he plowed through a wall of briars that only a thousand-pound horse could have managed, and a forest of massive cedars and oaks swallowed him. He waited in the carpet of needles under a twisted limb until the choppy whine died away, then fell off a limestone hogback and continued down the slope.

He found the canyon bottom flat and timbered, with small verdant meadows spangled with yellow flowers. Honey bees stirred from the blossoms as he passed and butterflies danced by in graceful flight. Thin trails in the grass told of jackrabbits and armadillos, and an oak sapling shorn of its bark marked the visit of a buck deer. From down-canyon came the call of a bob white quail, a two-note solo rising against the steady buzz of cicadas in the elms.

It was a wilderness, as pristine as if he had just ridden back through time. And again Charlie was at home, away from the nineteen nineties, corralled into the era in which he always had belonged. People were different back then, the old-timers had told him. They were big-hearted and honest, and if they weren't particularly religious, they at least had their own moral code of conduct. If a man shook hands on a deal, it meant more than his signature. If he told somebody he'd be somewhere at a certain time, a person could set his watch by it. If a stranger passed by his home at dusk, he invited him in for supper and lodging. And even if he went away for a while, he left the door unlocked and expected a passer-by to stop for the night and help himself to food and a bed. And all he expected in return was for the stranger to wash his own dishes and maybe leave a note. And a man knew how to treat a woman in those days, too, thought Charlie. Sure, a young cowboy starved for romance might pay a visit to the little house on the hill, but he damned sure respected a real lady. He knew better than to curse or make an improper remark around one, and he might never so much as even kiss the girl he loved until after they were married.

Yes, thought Charlie, it was a simpler era back then, and he could not understand why he had been denied it.

His ride through the past was broken again by the choppy whir of the helicopter, and he took the horse in under thick timber and stopped in the heavy shadows. Thorns rasped against his hat as he looked up to see patterned slivers of daylight through tangled briars that choked a leafy oak. The chopper was up there somewhere, intruding on his world, and had it been anybody but L. D. behind it, he would have hated him for it. As it was, he only felt sorry that the cowboy who had shared his JAs line camp and his dreams had climbed off his horse to let the world tell him just who and what he was to be.

Dismounting, he removed the bridle and slid it back on the bay's neck to wrap the reins around the saddle horn. Staking it with the catch-rope, he sat on deadfall to smoke and remember.

They had ridden up out of the JAs breaks—Charlie, L. D., and the squint-eyed, eighty-five-year-old cowboy named Tom—to turn their horses to the rim and look off the cap-rock at the sprawling canyon called Palo Duro. Far below, the coppery loam and sluggish waters of the Big Red snaked through a vast thicket guarded by buttes and bluffs.

"First time I've seen this country from a horse since they moved me out of Campbell Creek Camp," L. D. was saying.

He lifted his hat to let the up-drafting wind cool his sweaty hair. "Sure envy you boys gettin' to do it so much—up at headquarters they keep me in a pickup most of the time. They've had a damned hard time at roundup so far, though, tryin' to get me up in that helicopter—or on one of those two-wheeled noise-makers either one."

Charlie spat a brown stream of tobacco juice over the bluff. "That ain't no way for a cowboy to have to live, L. D.," he said quietly.

"They ain't no real cowboys no more, Roper," the old man offered, in a voice that quaked with the years. "Times won't allow 'em." He stretched a gnarled arm toward the rugged expanse below. "Take a look out there—when I first rode up to the JAs on a little iron-gray horse in nineteen sixteen this was a real outfit. They had a world of country, maybe a thousand sections the whole seventy miles from Amarillo to Memphis, and there was just three big pastures. They was twenty-five thousand mother cows to be worked and eighteen cowboys to do it, not countin' all the horse wranglers and hoodlum drivers, cooks and windmillers.

"I tell you, we done cow work then, day after day, winter and summer. We'd start out in April and brand all the range by the Fourth of July. Boy, when night come you was ready to go to bed; you'd flanked five hundred calves. Then they'd start out the fifteenth of September on the fall work and push those herds up to the railroad. A thunderstorm would come up and the lightning would be like a red ball of fire on your horse's ears, and then those cattle would go to runnin'. You take two thousand head of two-year-old steers, and when they break to run you can just hear that roarin'. Them ol' horses would just go wild—they'd jump and run at the same time the cattle would. You could feel your horse's heart a-beatin' against your leg.

"But that's how it was back then. We'd sleep out all year 'round, in teepees if it was a bad night rainin', and nobody ever complained, 'less somebody was to give you a bunch

of dogs to ride—you know, sorry old beat-out horses. See, a cowboy was a fellow that had a lot of self-respect and pride about his work—long as he had a good horse and a place to ride, well, that's all that mattered."

He paused to breathe deeply, and anger filled his voice. "Now look at it. From right here you can see the whole JAs, what's not leased out. We barely got a thousand mother cows and you got to go through six fences just to go the nine miles between headquarters and Campbell Creek Camp. Now they tell me they want to shut down my camp, let go a bunch of men, just drive over in a pickup ever' couple of days and honk the horn to get the cattle up."

Charlie reached down and rubbed his gelding's neck, letting his sweat mingle with the dampness on its coat. "They'll do it without me," he said quietly.

"Yeah, well, they'll do it with you or without you—way times are, don't s'pose they got any choice."

"Better face facts, Charlie," said L. D. "Man wants a job on a ranch these days, he's got to put his horse out to pasture and do what the boss says. I don't like it any better than you, but we better learn to adjust—or look for another line of work."

"Huh!" Charlie exhaled sharply. "Lookin' for work's one thing; findin' another way to live's somethin' else."

"Well, I'll tell both you boys somethin'," said Tom. "Those old days are gone, and we'll never see 'em again. I never have forgotten 'em either; the best years of my life was then, you know. They can say what they want to about these modern times; by gosh, people was happier then than they are now. Now you, L. D., I think'll do okay livin' somewheres else, makin' some other kind of livin'. But you, Roper, I don't know. You just gotta change with the times or they'll eat you up just like a cancer."

And all these years later, as Charlie ground the butt into the oak, he felt the cancer eating right through his heart.

Chapter Six

Hearing the helicopter continue to make passes through the canyon, Charlie risked unsaddling the bay to let it rest as it grazed, and waited with the patience of a man for whom time no longer had meaning. The sun crawled higher, altering the grid work of shadows on the ground, and finally began to fall toward the forested bluff that Charlie knew lay to the west-northwest. He ate twice and sipped from the water jug, and smoked a pack of cigarettes as he watched his horse swish its tail and paw and stomp at the ground. Charlie understood, and cared. Punished by thirst, it had reverted to the mustang's instinct to seek water in the cracks and mud of seemingly dry wallows.

It was not until the helicopter ceased its frequent passes and the shadows lengthened across the nearby meadow that Charlie saddled up and rode up-canyon. The thickening undergrowth and timber squeezed him down into the drainage, itself so tangled with protruding limbs and drift that Charlie paid the price in scrapes for being without leggings. As it was, he could only lean close to the gelding and let it plow through with a crisp snap of limbs and the musical strike of rocks kicked across limestone floor. Sometimes he broke through glistening spider webs suspended across the wash, while drift dams or deadfall cedars the size of a man's waist often forced him up the bank to pass.

He came upon a tarantula crawling up an oak on the bank, then a horned toad resting in the fork of a mesquite. And later, at the sudden staccato of maracas, he wheeled his spooked horse to avoid a rattlesnake dangling from an overhanging limb. And he remembered the "guaranteed sign" the old cowboys had passed along: *When ground species start taking to the trees, look for a gully washer in about three days.*

Far up-canyon in the narrows he came across a tinaja with oak leaves afloat in its shallows and let his horse drink. Day was fast dying now, and the shrill drone of locusts was giving way to the peaceful chirp of crickets. But it was another sound drifting down-canyon that suddenly stirred him, and he turned his face to the brush hugging the northwest slope and recognized the faraway snorting of a horse in distress.

A cowboy's inbreeding to defend the animal that made him what he was led Charlie to rein his mount up the bluff. Heavy brush turned him away, and he went farther along the drainage to the rising cry of the horse before he angled up the slope on a well-beaten game trail. He went up through rimrock and crashed through tangled undergrowth to burst onto a narrow, timbered ridge swelling against the great canyon wall. He came upon a barbed-wire fence rising against the brush and cursed it as it herded him up-canyon along its strands. If ever there had been one single thing that had destroyed the Old West and the need for a cowboy, it had been barbed wire.

Charlie rode into a slight wind that creaked boughs and rustled shrubs, which is probably why he came upon the scene he did. Where the timber ended near the canyon's rocky head, he looked down the cedar posts to see, fifty yards away, an upended Steel Dust colt pinned in the fence and flailing at the ground, blood streaming down a neck and shoulder and leg twisted in barbed wire. And off to the side, three coyotes with the lean look of hunger lunged in and out, snapping at the exposed flanks and dodging the thrashing hooves. Already, the pack had opened up a dozen bloody wounds, but the colt still had plenty of fight left.

Just like Charlie.

He fumbled with a box of cartridges, spilling more than he grasped, and loaded the twenty-two as he galloped his animal into the clearing. Seething with anger at a barbed-wire world, he cried out and shouldered the rifle as he rode half-blind into a sun setting behind rimrock ahead.

On the mesa top, they found where Charlie had trotted his horse through the cedar-flecked grassland, only to lose his trail in the table rock hugging the canyon that had separated him from the windmill. They spent futile hours trying to pick it up again before L. D. put a call through on the radio and they rode for the tower rising over the gorge. It was near that mill, confirmed the chopper crew, that they had glimpsed something at daybreak and later found stock tracks. Whether it was the trail of a horse bearing a rider, the two men had been unable to tell, and the additional officers dispatched by vehicle to the site had been turned back by impassable washouts.

In the pitted road that marked the last quarter-mile to the windmill, L. D. found tracks. He read them at a glance, but it was the old rancher who traced their course with a knotted finger.

"See how them shoes bit into the ground, how they're spaced out like they are? Somebody was durned sure astride that horse, all right, a-ridin' in a lope right for that mill."

"Yes, sir, Mr. McBee, I see it," L. D. said politely.

From two horses over, Syers breathed sharply. "All you damned ignorant country sheriffs know how to do is play hell, Hankins," he snapped. "They *had* that SOB. They had him and you let him get away. Or maybe that's the way you wanted it."

L. D.'s face flushed hot and he reined his horse sharply to the ranger, a torrent of invectives ready at his lips. But Fowler's outstretched hand stayed his words, and he looked to see sunlight glinting from the Jim Ned County sheriff's badge.

"Some people," said Fowler, turning to face Syers, "might call *me* a country sheriff, Gene."

Syers straightened in the saddle, his hard eyes narrowing behind the shades. "When I say something about somebody, I'm damned sure not afraid to call his name, so you can just stop pretending you're so riled up, Fowler. *Hankins* knows what I meant. How about you, Fowler, the rest of you people? Did you know what big friends he and this Lyles are?"

"L. D. will catch him, I guarantee you," Milton babbled excitedly. "It don't matter to him *who* it is, long as they broke the law."

L. D. breathed sharply, as much in disgust over his young deputy's constant need to defend him as in what Syers had said. But it was the ranger who caught his glare. "You feelin' uncomfortable about all this, Syers?" he asked. "About me bein' here, knowin' Charlie before? Well, I'll tell you, there's not a one of you understands him the way I do, not a one of you's got any idea what he's thinkin' and what he might do next but me. You think I like all this ridin' out here in the hot sun? I'll be damned glad to go back in and prop up my feet in front of the air conditioner. I'd just be tickled to be sittin' there drinkin' a cold beer and let *you* worry about findin' him."

A caustic half-laughed passed Syers' lips. "So what in the hell's this Lyles up to now? Better yet, why don't you just tell us where the hell he is."

L. D. slung a hand to the windmill ahead. "He carried a water jug so he didn't need water for himself, but he did for his horse. That's why he was headin' this way. When the chopper come over it turned him, and I bet he went off the other side down in the canyons again. He's off down there right now with a thirsty horse and wonderin' why the hell we won't just leave him alone. He's been lookin' for natural water today, but if he don't find any he'll be tryin' to get to a windmill come dark."

Syers cursed under his breath, but when L. D. rode on down the horseman's trail, he nevertheless followed with the others.

They found the chittam mott where Charlie's mount had thrown him, then after a long rest they trailed him back to the north through a grassy flat with prickly pear blooming orange and bear grass waving in the wind. Where the tracks were clear, L. D., Milton, and Powers rode abreast and talked about the ranger's wife and newborn son. But when the trail dimmed in the massing cedars, L. D. rode to the forefront to study the signs in the rocky turf. A chipped piece of slate, a rock dirty-side-up, a bleeding prickly pear, a bruised horse nettle, a freshly snapped limb—they all told the story of a horseman riding hard for the rim only to be turned up-canyon by a sheer drop. L. D. turned up-canyon with him, only to find solid table rock obscuring the trail. He knew that Charlie had dropped into the adjoining canyon, but at what point?

They discussed it as they rode into the steadily falling sun, and L. D. lagged to study the rim more carefully. Milton, now more sure of the reins, fell back with him, and the two of them went single-file along the drop-off just outside the irregular line of cedars. An updraft cooled the sweat on L. D.'s back, but now that he had turned into the sun it was like riding into a Dutch oven fire. The limestone shelf before him was like whitewash under its rays, and he rubbed his aching eyes and wished for even those blue-tinted driving shades Sarah had gotten him. Even worse, his neck and the part of his face unshaded by his hat brim burned like a hot branding iron, and he wondered if he were broiled like everyone else.

Five minutes came and went, with the other riders widening their lead and no trace of Charlie's passage turning up.

Then L. D., his eyes on the rim, straightened and slowed his horse to a stop. He looked around at Milton's lathered roan nodding along just ahead, and beyond his inattentive deputy at the rest of the party. One by one, they were disappearing where the rim cut back sharply into the timber. Then he looked again at the ledge, at the cedar guarding it from just below, at the brown strands of horsehair clinging to a dead limb and fluttering in the wind.

Horsehair so situated could mean only one thing—that a horse had descended that shelf. A horse had gone over there, *Charlie's* horse, and a limb had reached out and clawed it. And now the sign loomed plain for all to see.

But they hadn't. They had all ridden past, oblivious to it, and unless L. D. spoke up no one would ever know.

But wait—what made him so sure it had been Charlie's horse? After all, weren't there several other horses running free in this pasture? Hadn't they come across a couple on this very mesa? And anyway, wasn't McBee up ahead? He'd probably seen the horsehair and recognized it as the wrong shade of brown, so why waste everybody's time by calling them back now?

L. D.'s mind still churned like a West Texas dust devil when the creak of leather reached his senses. He turned to see Milton twisted around in the saddle, his eyes evidently fixed on that patch of horsehair playing in the wind. The youthful eyes came on around to catch L. D.'s, and for just a moment L. D. read the turmoil of a person balancing impropriety against trust, justice against friendship, disillusionment against admiration. And then without even so much as another glance at the cedar, Milton turned and urged his gelding forward.

L. D. swallowed hard, remembering the cowboy, and rode on.

As they scouted the rim far into the west, he tried to convince himself that he had not acted improperly, that, like a good investigator, he simply had recognized an obviously empty lead and passed on it. But, damn it, if that was the case, why the hell did he feel so guilty every time Milton looked at him?

The day wore on, extended and exhausting for both men and horses. They rested more frequently now, the men sipping from depleted canteens and nibbling on snacks while the animals pawed thirstily at the ground. Even L. D. sagged in the saddle before the miles and oppressive heat; repeatedly he found himself staring down blankly at his glistening rein hand, his head nodding in sleepy rhythm to the gentle rocking of his horse.

Finally one horse stopped and they all did, on a rocky, wind-swept point jutting out over canyon greenery.

Syers removed his hat to wipe his brow and curse. "We lost him. We lost the SOB."

"We sure lost his trail all right," said Fowler, glancing back up the rim.

Out of the corner of his eye, L. D. caught Milton slowly turning in his direction, and suddenly it was as if he could feel the stare piercing him through and through. He was staring, and L. D. couldn't make himself look back.

"Sure would like to get back to that boy of mine before he gets out of the crib," Powers said tiredly, rubbing a knee. "Longest day I ever spent, except when he was born. Sheriff Hankins, what's your guess as to where Lyles went?"

L. D. shifted in the saddle to ease the pressure on his thighs. "I still think he may be comin' after water when it starts gettin' dark. Mr. McBee, there a windmill down in that canyon?"

The old man spat a stream of tobacco juice down by his horse's front hoof. "Not any that's still a-workin'. Gotta get up on top somewheres for one of those."

L. D. squinted into the falling sun ahead. "That a mill tower I see over there on the horizon? It still work?"

"Mighty gyppy, but she still pumps."

"Got a road to it?"

"Same one as goes to the first one. Forks up a ways. Them boys said it was washed out pretty bad in a spot or two."

L. D. nodded. "The horses'd be able to trail it back in to the highway in the dark, wouldn't they? Tell y'all what: sundown's comin' pretty fast, and we're all gonna be caught out here not able to see each other, much less somebody hidin'. Let's take a gamble on him comin' up that bluff at dusk, waterin' his horse the first mill he sees. If we don't see anything, we can ride back on in. If we do, we got him."

And as they began riding, too tired to grumble, into the ever-sinking sun, a single, guilt-laden thought filled L. D.'s mind: *Don't come up that bluff, Charlie. For God's sake, don't come up.*

The rim and depths stayed alongside all the way to the canyon head, where the horses picked their way down into a rocky gully thick with stunted cedars. Twenty yards to the right, great outcrops of limestone guarded a pour-off, falling away in stair steps, and framed the folds of the canyon staggering toward distant buttes.

Down and away from the pillared rock on the left, a hundred yards or more, a ridge stood bare against the great timbered bluff—and on it, suddenly, L. D. caught quick movement. A split second of confusion slowed his reactions, dulled his speech, and his hand seemed to rise toward it in slow-motion, his lips straining to form words that loomed as distant as a past century. Then Syers took up the cry, pointing and cursing, and suddenly a half-dozen horses wheeled to fight for footing.

"There's the SOB!" shouted the ranger, and all eyes became fixed on the oncoming horseman who leaned into his bay's shoulders to take it up the ridge. The horse came galloping at such an angle that within seconds the outcrop would hide rider and animal.

"Bastard's lifting his rifle!" cried Syers, and simultaneously came the crack of a firearm from down in the canyon. L. D. whirled just in time to see Syers shoulder his .223

Ruger and fire, the barrel swinging with the flight of the horseman, the *rat-a-tat-tat* of a dozen quick rounds singing out in staccato to end in the whizzing of ricocheting slugs as outcrop exploded. The rapid burst of gunfire spooked the horses, and as L. D. fought to keep his animal's head up, he glimpsed Powers slumping in his saddle. For an instant he took it as an inexperienced rider trying to cope with a skittish horse, then he realized something was terribly wrong. For Powers laid his head, almost gently, across his animal's neck and began to slide, smearing blood all the way down the gelding's shoulder as he fell in a heap to its hooves.

"He's hurt!" cried L. D., wheeling his animal to see hooves pawing at the man's head. "Get that horse off of him!"

Syers, oblivious to all but the cowboy on the ridge, had spurred his animal to the brink of the pour-off and readied his Ruger again. But Fowler, nearest the riderless horse, lunged for the reins and finally clutched the bridle down close to the bit. At the same time, L. D. and Milton were springing from their mounts, leaving McBee to follow after their wandering horses.

"Horse split open his neck, L. D.!" cried Milton as they fell to the prostrate man.

"Hell, he's been shot!" shouted Fowler.

Powers lay face down, blood massing under his right ear to pool on the rock basin. He lay very still, and as L. D. cupped the warm forehead pillow-like and pressed a stifling palm against the oozing wound, he remembered Powers' wife and baby.

Good God, Charlie, he thought. *Good God.*

Chapter Seven

The sights wavered violently down the rifle barrel as Charlie rocked to the lunging gallop that flung turf with each thud of his horse's hooves. He found a coyote face-to-face through the sights and fired, discharging the weapon directly between the gelding's ears. The horse swerved sharply at the report and a bullet whizzed by Charlie, and as the momentum of the spooked animal carried them on up the ridge, a quick dozen puffs of dust raced alongside at the base of the fence.

The burst of semi-automatic gunfire still echoed down-canyon when Charlie thundered past the pinned colt to scatter the coyotes into the brush. Whirling to the rimrock at the canyon head, he saw nothing but the brilliance of the setting sun. Then he too gained the timber, to look back at the injured colt and curse those forcing him to ride away and let it die in the barbs.

Cutting through the fence, he turned the horse up the rising bluff and spurred it back down-canyon through heavy oaks and cedars tangled with undergrowth. He didn't know where the gunfire had come from, or why; all he knew was that he was mad, damned mad. Shielded, he looked down as he crossed above the bare ridge and his anger rose at the sight of the thickening blood at the colt's hindquarters; the animal still thrashed helplessly at ground already red-splattered. When dark fell, Charlie knew, the coyotes would return, to rip and tear in a cruel, slow torture that finally would see it bleed to death.

The hell they will! he cried silently.

And taking swift aim, he ended the colt's misery with a *crack!* and a bullet through the skull.

Then he was off, plowing the horse through thorny vines that would have snared a weaker horse. He urged the animal on with occasional slaps on the neck all the way along the jungled slope until the swell below grew wooded, then found a deer trail and angled down to cut through the fence again and gain the canyon floor. As he turned the horse down the dusky drainage, he twisted around to see the forested rim at the canyon head as a toothy silhouette against the red sky. And his slow words came in a raspy whisper.

"'Member chousin' that old horned cow that time, L. D.? How she finally turned and ripped your horse's belly plum' open? If I hadn't've dragged her off with my catch-rope, she'd've done the same thing to you.

"Keep chousin' me this way, L. D., backin' me in a corner and shootin' at me, and you're gonna make me turn on you just like that old cow—only this time there ain't gonna be nobody to drag me—"

He started at sudden gunfire that cut out half the tree above and set his horse bolting. Leaves came drifting down like snow, but he already was whirling at the animal's quick lunge to hug its neck and spur it down-canyon.

Brush cracked and splintered before the gelding's onrush into the gloom, but Charlie, feeling the rifle tight in his hand, suddenly felt an even greater darkness inside.

For he knew L. D. had finally backed him into that corner—he had no choice now but to fight back.

No sooner had L. D. placed caring hands at Powers' head than the man died, in a convulsive gasp that smeared both their shirts red.

He didn't have to slide his fingers around to the carotid artery, but he did anyway. And, strangely, it was Sarah he thought of, Sarah and the baby she kept talking about having. He had resisted up to now because he was still too restless, still longing for all those dreams he was letting slip away. But he could damn sure picture her with a little baby to take care of while he lay out here dead in his own blood.

"He killed him, L. D., he killed him. You let him go and he killed him."

L. D. looked up from where he knelt still supporting Powers' head to see Milton, pale and gape-jawed, breathing in short spurts as he stretched a trembling arm to the body. The deputy found blood and pulled his hand away, turning it to see his wavering fingertips moist and red against bone-white bedrock.

Only now did the eyes shift to L. D., and they were the disillusioned eyes of one knowing betrayal. "They all said you wanted him to get away; they all said it and I kept taking up for you." His bloody hand stole outward and the fingers closed on L. D.'s arm. "You rode right on by, L. D.; you rode right on by and he killed him."

L. D. jerked his arm free. "Get the hell away from me, Milton," he snapped. He lowered the dead man's head and stood, feeling the blood sticky on his hands. Movement in the notched rimrock down and away from Milton caught his vision, and he watched Syers rein his horse about and heard the sudden curse as the eyes fell to the bloodied drainage bed.

"What happened to Powers?" Syers asked coldly.

Fowler, still mounted, looked up as his horse shifted with the restless stirring of the riderless animal. "Shot."

"Bad?"

Fowler's horse spun away. "Enough," he said, wheeling the animal and finding L. D.'s eyes, "to make that bastard just another cop killer like all the rest."

L. D. turned away to lower his head and rasp a hand across his face. He could see Milton's bloody fingerprints streaking his upper sleeve. *Good God, Charlie*, he thought, *you've gone and killed a man. I didn't go after you and now you've gone and killed a man.*

And not just any man. L. D. was a sheriff now, not a cowboy, and Charlie had killed one of L. D.'s own—a public servant, a law enforcement officer, a Texas Ranger.

And a husband and father.

Good God, Charlie, how could you have done it? Don't you know it's me up here, puttin' my butt on the line for Sarah and the county for a couple of thousand a month? How the hell could you go and start shootin' like that?

Behind him the others milled around half-stunned, shock and anger filling their words. He heard his own name bandied about a couple of times. Hell, could he blame them, when a man was lying there dead because of him?

Replaying it all in his mind, he lifted his eyes from boots to scattered rocks to pour-off and up the pillared outcrops. And he remembered the sounds: Syers' quick cry. The *ping!* of a rifle down in the canyon. The burst of semi-automatic gunfire. The shattering of rock outcrop. The whiz of ricocheting bullets. The jingle of spurs as Powers crumpled to the bedrock.

Furrows dug into his brow, and he went closer to the pour-off, picturing again that horseman riding like hell up that slope, riding in full gallop and shouldering a rifle seemingly off-target *and still felling a man at a hundred yards through a narrow cleft.*

And in a stark revelation that set his heart hammering, he knew Powers hadn't died by Charlie's hand, *but by a ricocheting bullet from Syers' own Ruger.*

He knew it. Damn it, he knew it beyond a shadow of a doubt. What he didn't know, though, was why the hell he hadn't figured it out sooner, considering that the twenty-two shells Charlie had taken from that wetback shack couldn't have torn Powers' neck open that way.

He whirled to the others, but the words at his lips died in the sudden *ping!* of a rifle again from down in the canyon.

"Look out!" cried Milton, falling away. "He's gonna shoot us all!"

Syers reined his horse sharply up the opposite bank. "I'm going down after the SOB!"

"Let's hit it!" shouted Fowler, releasing Powers' horse to spur his own after the ranger.

"Kill him!" yelled Milton. "Kill the SOB!"

"Hey! Y'all wait a minute! You hear me?" L. D.'s voice was lost in the clomp of hooves. "He's not the one shot Powers! I said hold up!"

Suddenly, Milton too was mounted, gripping the saddle horn and brushing past L. D. to turn the roan up the incline after the disappearing riders. Flushed with frustration and anger, L. D. lunged for the bridle, spooking the animal enough to set it pitching. Panicking, Milton lasted only four jumps before he tumbled hard to the ground, and L. D. didn't take time to help him up. Stumbling over his outstretched legs, L. D. seized the reins and then was astride the animal, touching it with his spurs and feeling its power as it carried him up the bank.

He came eye-level with the mesa and looked through the gangly, striding legs of Fowler's horse as it veered toward the canyon; he could see a dismounting Syers momentarily framed at the rim sixty yards away. Then the roan gained the flat, a dozen lengths behind the brown gelding that separated him from the ranger stumbling down a break in the rimrock.

"Hey!" cried L. D. "Fowler! Get him stopped!"

Fowler turned in the saddle, catching L. D.'s eyes, then pushed harder for the rim and riderless horse.

"I said call him back!" yelled L. D.

Again his words went unheeded, and L. D. slapped the roan on the neck to close the gap in moments with superior horsemanship. Fowler, sensing the onrush, glanced around, and just as the roan was about to thunder by, he turned his horse directly into L. D.'s path.

The roan snorted and reared, pawing at the sky, and only L. D.'s quick anticipation kept him in the saddle. He got the animal under control and whirled to Fowler. "What the hell you doin'?" he cried angrily.

"Just hold on now, Sheriff," snapped Fowler. He slung his head toward the bloody arroyo. "I think maybe you better sit this one out."

L. D. spurred his horse. "The hell with what you think! Get out of my way!"

The roan caught Fowler hard in the thigh as it brushed past, and another few strides took it to the drop-off. L. D. hesitated just long enough to scout the shadowy slope, then he let the animal gingerly pick its way down through the break in the rimrock. The decline was severe, the footing poor on unstable rock and sloughing tiers, but they went crashing down through cedars and briars to find the forested upper section of the ridge. They came up alongside a barbed-wire fence, and L. D. slowed long enough to look down the strands and see Syers running in a crouch into the clearing, the .223 Ruger fierce in his hands.

"Hyahhh!" L. D. encouraged his horse through the timber with a cry and the touch of spurs, and they exploded into the open just in time to see Syers shoulder the rifle and take aim deep into the canyon. The roan shied at the *rat-a-tat-tat* of semi-automatic gunfire, but L. D. pushed it on at break-neck speed straight for the narrow gap between Syers and the fence line. The ranger popped in another clip, then the roan barrelled past and L. D. leaned out to knock the weapon viciously from his hands.

He reined his horse to a stop, just short of the now-stilled colt, and wheeled about through a storm of dust to see Syers flushed with rage.

"Just listen for a minute, damn it, listen!" cried L. D., turning his hand palm-up in a half-plea.

Syers levied on him some of the vilest invectives L. D. had ever heard and began gesturing wildly as he stalked around the roan. He cursed and raved threateningly for half a minute before he finally calmed enough for a quiet, caustic laugh.

"So it's not enough for that bastard buddy of yours to be a cop killer headed for lethal injection if I don't gut-shoot him first—looks like there's going to be a two-bit SOB of a sheriff doing some time of his own for obstructing justice." And he glanced at the rifle in the dirt.

L. D. made sure to keep his hand clear of his .357 and any gestures that could be misconstrued as hostile.

"All I'm stoppin' is a *miscarriage* of justice—and I'll damned sure do what I have to to do it, too. Yeah, there's a man lyin' dead back there, a damned good one with a wife and kid and a bullet hole through his neck. But just pick that rifle up—pick the damned thing up, you hear me? I want you to hold it and run your fingers down the barrel and tell me what it feels like to kill a man with it. Go on! Tell me what it feels like to take a daddy away from his little boy the rest of his life."

"What the hell are you talking about?"

"I'm sayin' Charlie Lyles didn't no more shoot Powers than I did. I'm sayin' it was a bullet from your own Ruger bouncin' off that rock that blew a hole through his neck."

Syers' eyes closed to slits and he spoke through clenched teeth. "You know what *I'm* saying? That you're a lying SOB who'd do anything to make sure that friend of yours gets away. I'm telling you right now, Hankins—he's not going to do it. He got away again this time, but I swear I'll gut-shoot him tomorrow, or the day after that. He's a cop killer—and now he's going to die for it."

L. D. looked at the rifle, still on the ground. "I want that Ruger, Syers. I'm gettin' an autopsy done, ballistic tests run on that rifle. I'll damn sure show the world how Powers *really* died. Just show me a twenty-two that can make a hole that big in a man's neck."

Syers cursed him again. "A lawman's supposed to find facts—not make them up. Nobody ever said he's got a twenty-two rifle—that wetback couldn't tell a twelve gauge shotgun from a cannon."

"He took all those twenty-two shells—what do you think that was for?"

Syers slapped the holster of his forty-five automatic. "Probably has a pea-shooter, a sidearm."

"I saw him shoulder a rifle and fire—it had the sound of a twenty-two."

"What the hell makes *you* such a firearms expert?" demanded Syers. "The humidity and lay of the land and even time of day affect how a rifle sounds—that could've been anything, a 30-30, a 30.06, maybe even another Ruger. The hell with your ballistics tests and autopsy—I don't need anything but my own eyes to tell me there's a dead ranger back there and a cop killer in the canyon that's going to die for it."

L. D. motioned to the rifle and then slung his hand toward the gloomy brakes below. "Take it then! Go on—take it and go traipsin' off out there on foot in the dark if you want him so bad! But just remember, you come back and that thing goes to *me*. I don't care if you're a Texas Ranger or the governor himself—if you want to start a stink about obstructin' justice, just try keepin' that thing out of my hands."

Syers brooded for long moments, studying the rifle at his feet and the dusky canyon below. Finally, with a sharp breath, he angrily snatched the weapon from the ground and headed back for the rimrock.

L. D. sat watching until the shadowy timber hid the ranger, then sucked in air deeply and turned away, plagued by self-doubts. His eyes caught the dead colt wrapped in the fence, and curiosity prompted him to rein his horse closer. Up to now, he had been too preoccupied with Syers to pay it any mind, but now he quickly read the story of an animal that had been hopelessly caught in slashing barbs. But there was something else he saw in the twilight, and he climbed off the roan to find canine tracks splattered with fresh blood.

Frowning, he stretched an arm through the fence and ran a hand along the animal's still-sweaty nose, and when he found the fresh bullet wound above the eyes he stood back and swallowed hard. His fingers shook as he pieced it all together, and he clenched them against a sudden chill and stared into the dusk that shrouded the canyon floor.

Good God, Charlie, couldn't you have let him suffer just this once? Why'd you have to go liftin' that rifle, makin' everybody think you was shootin' at us? Now they'll say you did it, Charlie; they'll say you're a cop killer. And if I can't prove it different, if I can't make 'em believe it before they catch up to you, they'll kill you for it.

And hearing the sudden snort of a horse from down-canyon, L. D. turned his eyes toward it and a silent cry exploded from the wellsprings of his spirit. *Ride, Charlie— ride like hell!*

Chapter Eight

L. D. carried the morbid image with him all the way back to the Sims County sheriff's office.

Powers' body. Draped face-down across a horse. Swaying with every stride through the night.

They had laid him there like a sack of feed, his arms and legs dangling down the bay's rib cage, and had joined his wrists to his ankles by a leather cord girded tight across the animal's underside.

And they had brought him back to a widow and her fatherless child.

Sitting at his paper-cluttered desk, L. D. massaged tired, burning eyes with a thumb and forefinger. He had a terrific headache, aggravated by the glare from the overhead light. He had never felt so physically and emotionally drained, and all he wanted to do was find energy enough to drag himself out of the chair and go home and never come back.

The sound of something heavy slamming against the desk top stirred him. He found the glint of the ceiling light in the metal of a .223 rifle, and he looked up past the withdrawing hand to find Syers' hardened eyes.

"Want to know what you can do with this thing?" snapped the ranger.

Flushing hot, L. D. grated his chair back and stood to face him across the desk. "Maybe you're fixin' to tell me," he challenged.

Syers breathed sharply, and his words came through clenched teeth. "You talk tough for nothing but a fat slob; now let's see how well you listen. Tomorrow I'm going back out and bringing that SOB in, and if it's the same way we did Powers—all the better. So get this straight—you're not showing your damned face anywhere near those canyons. You can go play with your rifle or your autopsy or that red-head over at the cafe, but just stay the hell away from me."

L. D. shook his head. "This is my county, Syers. You think I'd sit around up here and let you go get somebody else hurt and killed, like Milton over there or Fowler?"

The ranger glanced at the two men who stood leaned over topographic maps at the other end of the room, then half-laughed. "Open your damned eyes, Hankins. They both know what happened—that friend of yours out-and-out murdered a man and all you're trying to do is keep us from catching him."

L. D. looked at Fowler, who had raised his head at the mention of his name. "That what you're thinkin', Ernest?"

The Jim Ned County sheriff straightened and turned toward them. "Maybe you're a little too close to all of this. Maybe it'd be better if you did stay away tomorrow."

"So you don't think for a minute that maybe I'm right, that maybe Charlie didn't kill him after all."

Fowler took a weary breath. "Hell, I'm not a judge or jury, and I'm too tired to think anyway. But as tangled up in barbed wire as you say that colt was, it's no wonder he had cuts on his face. And all that ricocheting business . . . " He shook his head and sighed deeply. "A man would have to want to believe something else awfully bad not to face up to facts. All I know is Lyles went to shooting and Powers fell over dead. If I *was* the jury, that'd be facts enough for me."

"Listen, Ernest, I—"

"I've had enough for the night," Fowler said impatiently, turning to the door. "I'm going to the motel, get some rest."

L. D. exhaled in disgust and looked back at the rifle. Syers laughed lowly. "You can't even convince yourself of it, can you, Hankins. You want to, but you can't."

L. D. found his eyes. "I wonder what it's gonna do to the career of a ranger when it comes out he killed a man through negligence. Maybe when we're horseback tomorrow we can figure it out."

Syers' cheek began twitching and he stuck a finger in L. D.'s chest. "Don't get in my way again, Hankins. You get between my rifle and that SOB and I'll cut you in half the same as I will him."

With dull eyes L. D. watched Syers wheel and follow Fowler to the door, and as it screeched shut he shifted his attention to Milton, who still leaned over the table of maps. L. D. knew that his deputy realized his stare, but not once in all the long seconds of scrutiny did Milton give the slightest glance in his direction.

With a sigh of disgust, L. D. again sank into his chair and reached for the phone; he still had to make arrangements for the autopsy and ballistic tests with laboratories two hundred fifty miles away in Dallas, and with a local veterinarian to dig that slug out of that colt once the manhunt was over. Plus, there were those vulture-like reporters who had hovered around all day long and now seemed determined to call throughout the night.

Twenty minutes later, he found a deep breath and went wearily toward the door. Only now did Milton look up, and when L. D. came abreast, the younger man straightened and reached for his shoulder.

"L. D., you . . . you gave me a job when I needed one real bad." He swallowed hard and lowered his eyes. "I-I need it just as bad right now, L. D. I just got scared out there, said some things I didn't mean."

Hell, thought L. D., did he have to come sidling up that way just to save his damned job?

"You meant it, Milton," he snapped, brushing past.

But as he found the night beyond the door, he just hoped to hell Milton hadn't been right.

Sarah met him with a tender hand on his upper arm the moment he walked through the front door of their home. "I just caught the news over the radio—they say he killed a man, L. D., a *ranger*."

Impatiently, he flicked the door backwards, leaving it ajar, and walked on through her would-be embrace. "They're sayin' that, all right."

"Did he, L. D.?" she asked, securing the door and turning to study him.

L. D. plopped down on the sofa. Damn, he was tired. "Hell, I don't know. I don't know nothin' anymore."

Sarah came closer, concern lining her face. "I heard a Jim Ned deputy got hurt, too."

"Fractured his leg two places," he droned. "Just talked to the hospital over in San Angelo. They're keepin' him overnight."

"What *happened* out there today, darlin'?"

He looked at her earnestly. "It's just like I told 'em, just what I said all along. He's home out there, Sarah, and there ain't a one of us—me included—that stands a chance of gettin' by half as good as he does in all those canyons. Yeah, they're sayin' he killed a man, and come mornin' they'll all be out shootin' anything that moves. And there ain't no way in hell I can stop 'em."

Sarah went to him, to sit at his side and place a tender, concerned hand once more on his shoulder. "I know it's awful hard on you, L. D., tryin' to make yourself believe he could do somethin' like that."

He whirled to her and breathed sharply. "Damn it, Sarah, you're as bad they are. Charlie didn't kill *nobody*. That ranger had to be killed by a ricochet—one of our own bunch's. But damned if I can get anybody to believe it."

"Are you sure? Are you really sure?"

He sighed and looked down at his boots, which now had lost their luster. He shrugged. "I shouldn't *hafta* be the one to say, anyway—and not any of those yahoos that'll be running wild tomorrow either. What the hell's a judge for anyhow, or a jury? Yeah, if Charlie ever got his day in court, they might see it my way, all right. Thing is, when mornin' breaks, it's gonna be shoot to kill—and Charlie won't ever *get* that day."

"Isn't there something you can do, call off the manhunt or something?"

He shook his head. "Too late for that. There's been a man killed, a Texas Ranger, and even if I pulled the county off of it, there's too many other agencies out there with blood in their eye. Way I see it, I got just one chance. I've got to find Charlie before they do, else they'll out-and-out murder him for something he might not've done." He breathed deeply. "I'm diggin' my old bedroll out of the closet, packin' me a few eats. I'm goin' back out there tomorrow, Sarah, and I ain't comin' back in till I've found him."

Her hand stole up around his neck, and suddenly there was a quiver at her chin and great emotion in her voice. "Oh L. D., can't you just let what's gonna happen, happen? If he's out there with a gun and knows they're out to kill him, he's liable to do anything to get away." He turned to see her swallow hard. "*Anything*, L. D. . . . even to you."

L. D. found her hand, and squeezed it tightly. "The cowboy'd do the same for me, Sarah. I know damned well he would."

But deep inside, he wondered if Sarah were right.

L. D. forced himself to shower away the dried sweat and trail dust, and he was still sitting at the kitchen table forcing down a reheated supper when the telephone rang. As Sarah started for it in the living room, he gently caught her by the arm. "If it's any more of those damned reporters, I'm not here," he said tiredly.

Watching her walk away, he slumped in his chair and closed his eyes for long seconds. He could still feel the rocking gait of a horse, still see its head nodding endlessly before him.

"L. D., I think you oughta come talk."

He looked up to find her framed in the open doorway. "Who is it?"

"Some friend of Charlie Lyles. Says she's just got to talk to you."

L. D. breathed deeply and shook his head. "Tell her I can't right now. Tell her I've gotta get some sleep."

"But darlin', she says she saw Charlie just a couple of days ago."

L. D. straightened. He scooted back his chair and stood. "Couple of days?" He made his way past her into the living room to reach for the receiver on the small table aglow in lamplight.

"This is L. D.," he said, sinking into an easy chair.

Through a crackling line denoting great distance he heard the slow and wavering words of an elderly woman. "Sheriff Hankins, they say you're after Charlie Lyles, that you're hunting him down with guns and all. Don't hurt him. Please don't hurt him."

"Who is this?"

"He's a good person. He don't mean to hurt anybody."

"Yes, ma'am, I know that."

"He don't even know a stranger. He'd give him the shirt off his back if he needed it. If he tells you somethin's so, you can believe it's that a-way. And women, I never saw him show any kind of disrespect around one, no curse words or anything."

"Yes, ma'am, he's a cowboy," L. D. said simply, knowing that said it all.

He heard a half-sob and a plea fill her voice. "You won't hurt him, will you? You'll see to it that he don't get hurt?"

L. D. swallowed hard. "I'll sure do my best—you can count on it. Now, please, tell me who you are."

"I live down in Cedarville in the Hill Country. I'm Mrs. Willard Gideon. Charlie was just down here, staying with us. He was 'Roper' to me. I know a few months ago they had him in Huntsville, but he was a real good prisoner, else he wouldn't have got out quick as he did. He wasn't no outlaw or bandit to me or my family. See, I live with my daughter and son-in-law, and all five of my grandchildren just took up with him like they'd knowed him all their life. They all went swimming together, and then we drove around in the hills, and he even caught a bull snake and my oldest grandson made a pet out of it.

"I didn't have no idea Roper was in trouble. He never was one much for talking. But I just like the boy for what he is inside, not for what he's done. I know the Good Lord's got a place for cowboys, even cowboys like Roper."

"Yes, ma'am, I like to believe that, too." L. D. found his own voice strangely gripped by emotion.

"He was grateful for ever' bite we fed him, and I gave him two pairs of pants and three or four shirts, and tried to get him to take a pair of cowboy boots. The ones he was wearin' was all split down the front, but he said that's the way he liked them and that he never wore a pair of boots he didn't cut and lace up."

"Yes, ma'am, one time a horse fell with him way out in the pasture. His foot swelled up so bad, he couldn't get his boot off till he rode back in and somebody cut it off. He wanted to make sure it never did happen again."

"You know Roper, then."

"Yes, ma'am, we used to cowboy together."

"Then you ought to know what he's like. You know, all the time he was here, he just kept talking about coming back here and live, if he could just get some things straightened out. But he was real set on seeing his mother, so he left out hitchhiking up that way Monday morning. Seemed real important that he talk to her and get some things thrashed out in his head. When he left out on the road, the last thing he said was how that someday soon when he decided to settle down, he was coming back to Utopia and spend the rest of his life. Utopia's a little town just north of here in the hills."

"You say Monday morning, Mrs. Gideon?"

"About seven-thirty. Please don't let anybody hurt him. He deserves better."

"He sure does, ma'am. I 'ppreciate you callin'."

Sarah was before him when he hung up the phone and stood. "Let's go to bed," he told her. "You gotta help me get up real early, 'bout three-thirty."

"Darlin', that don't even give you four hours' sleep."

"I know. I gotta drive over to Walnut Canyon and then be back on the Divide ready to ride by daybreak."

"What's in Walnut Canyon, L. D.? That's not even your jurisdiction."

"Charlie's mother lives there. I gotta go talk to her."

"But you said Jim Ned County tried to serve a warrant on him there Tuesday and he wasn't there."

L. D. nodded. "I don't think he was then. I think he got there after that, and that somethin' awful must've happened to set him off the way he did." He glanced at the phone and related the gist of the conversation, then found a deep breath and shook his head. "I don't know what it was happened at his mother's, but somethin' damned sure grabbed him by the throat and wouldn't let loose till he took that horse. He was too close to bein' happy down there in Cedarville for it not to have."

Sarah placed a tender hand on his arm. "Can't it just wait, L. D? You're exhausted—you need sleep, all you can get. Is there anything that you can find out there that's going to help you catch up with him?"

He took a deep breath, and remembered again a thousand days riding side-by-side with the cowboy. "No, but maybe it'll help me understand him. Nobody else ever even tried to."

Chapter Nine

Nightfall and the tranquility of the crickets carried Charlie away from the helicopters and automatic weapons and men bent on hunting him down. He rode free under a jeweled sky, a cowboy once more in his element. He turned his horse up slopes loose with rock and rimmed with ledges, crossed grassy veldts by starlight, fell off into rocky canyons so dark he could see only the nodding of his animal's head before him. And memories rode alongside him every step.

They were mostly of his grandfather's uncle, what little he could remember of him, and of the little grave inside the rusted iron pickets back of the old house down in Walnut Canyon. He had only seen him that one time as a six-year-old, a feeble old man sitting there shaking on a hot summer day despite a lap blanket draped down his legs. Even at that, Charlie probably wouldn't have remembered him except that the old man had died that night and they had buried him a day or two later out beside the little depression with the big rock at its head. He remembered the man with the dark suit and wind-blown Bible nodding toward the smaller grave and talking, something about the lifelong sufferings of the old man in losing his wife and seeing illness snatch away his little boy's rightful chance to live. And then as the dust devil had come howling through, whipping the freshly turned dirt, the dark-suited man had muttered a few words about there being some things that just weren't meant to be understood.

Or maybe it just took thirty-two years to understand them, thought Charlie.

Friday, June 4

About midnight the moon rose through filtering cedars hugging cross-canyon rimrock, and Charlie came upon a screeching windmill on a plateau to water his horse and refill his jug. Then he was astride the animal again, trampling the twentieth century under its hooves, tasting real life for the first time ever. He chased the northern horizon into another etched canyon where, far in the night, he unsaddled and staked the gelding to let it graze a grassy clearing. As he sat on deadfall and smoked, he ran his fingers along the rifle's rust-caked barrel and lifted his eyes back to the south.

"Just back on off, L. D.," he whispered. "You know there ain't no turnin' back for me now." The memories of a miscast life suddenly choked him, and he stroked the trigger guard and clenched the weapon fiercely. "There never was."

L. D. slept only fitfully and awakened before the alarm went off. He slipped quietly out of Sarah's sleeping embrace and sat up, only to see her stir. He studied her curled up in the sheets and strangely thought of Powers, who similarly had lain before him just hours before, a new father anxious to know the love of his child, yet forever denied it by the dark, sticky pool beneath him. And suddenly L. D. considered how narrow-minded it was of himself to arbitrarily surrender a chance to be called Daddy, especially when Sarah yearned so much for a child herself. And as she reached for him and spoke his name, a half-sob of worry in her throat, he pulled her close to feel her warmth through the silky texture of her gown.

"When all this is over, Sarah," he whispered, "we're gonna talk some about addin' on that new little room you been wantin'."

And then he was up and gone.

The route to Walnut Canyon carried L. D. out on Highway 2038 and up on the Divide, where he skirted first the turnoff to the McBee line-camp shack and then the sentried pasture gate where the whole bizarre episode had started. As he drove on westward into the night, passing the patrolling DPS unit and negotiating the game wardens' roadblock, he became further convinced that something in Walnut Canyon had triggered Charlie's actions. The logistics were just too right, with only thirty miles separating the Lyles place from the line camp, and Walnut Canyon Road and Highway 2038 providing a direct line of travel.

Damn it, Charlie, he thought, *you came walkin' out of your mother's home all tore up and you hit this highway and just took the first horse you saw. And I'm gonna find out why.*

L. D. had never met Mrs. Lyles; he wasn't even sure that was her actual name, she had lived with so many men over the years. But he had driven the caliche road through Walnut Canyon often enough to be familiar with her place, and four-thirty A.M. found him at the door of a dark and sagging two-story house set down along the canyon's brushy arroyo.

A long minute of intermittent knocking finally brought a stirring inside. A light went on and the hoarse, sleepy drone of a woman's voice sounded through the door. "Who the hell is it. It's four o'clock in the mornin'."

"L. D. Hankins, ma'am, with the sheriff's department over in Sims County. I'm a friend of Charlie's. Sorry to be botherin' you so early, but I need to talk to you if I can."

"He ain't here. Y'all done been over and tried to arrest him."

"Yes, ma'am, that wasn't me. Charlie's in some trouble and I'm tryin' to help him out."

A curtain in the window moved and the wooden door opened to frame a haggard woman with wild, stringy hair and the puffy, etched face of an alcoholic. She stood hunched over, clutching a tattered robe at her breast and legs. "Radio says he killed a cop and hid himself out in the canyons."

"Well, that's what I'm tryin' to figure out."

She turned and slunk back inside, leaving the wooden door ajar. "Let him rot out there for all I care."

L. D. hesitated, then opened the screen and followed her into a room that was shadowy except for the light falling through an open doorway beyond. She went over and sat in an easy chair with leaking cotton filling, reached for a pack of cigarettes from a lamp table, and lit a smoke. Ill at ease, L. D. glanced around for a proper place to sit and finally pulled a straight chair up before her. The woman even now reeked of whiskey, and despite her seemingly demure actions at first, she let the robe split brazenly at her thighs as she leaned back to puff on the cigarette.

"Ma'am, you seen Charlie since those Jim Ned deputies was here?"

She drew on the cigarette that she held in the fork of her fingers, and, with the same quivering hand, swept the hair out of her face. "Got rid of the no-'count bastard for good this time."

"Then he *was* here, knows about the warrant. He have some kind of rifle with him?" The moment he voiced the question, his mind reverberated with a silent plea. *A twenty-two—for God's sake, tell me it was a twenty-two!*

She flicked the cigarette ashes into a fruit jar lid on the lamp table. "Pried the hasp off the shed out back. I wouldn't give him the key. Don't know what all the bastard had in there."

She took another deep drag and tossed her head to the side, exhaling a funnel of smoke. "He don't belong here— he never did," she droned quietly, as if to herself, without ever turning her hardened, bloodshot eyes back to L. D. "I told him that mornin' what my sister done. I told him how 'fore he was born I'd catch her beatin' on herself with rocks and how I'd take 'em away from her. The thing just wouldn't die. It kept right on growin' in her, when all she wanted to do was get rid of it. Nobody knows how I've wished to hell, ever' since, that I'd let her done it, 'cause of the way he ended up killin' her, just bein' borned.

"Wasn't no father, so there I was, had to take him in like he was my own, seein' her and blamin' myself ever' time I looked at the spiteful little bastard."

She had a damned callous way of telling it, thought L. D., *even to a total stranger. What about to Charlie? But hell, maybe Charlie had already known she wasn't his real mother. And anyway, could finding out he was never wanted have shaken him so, considering he had never known a mother's love? How could it have broken a man so near happiness just a day before in the Hill Country? More, there had to be more.*

She tapped the ashes from the cigarette with an index finger. "Other mornin', he started in askin' me all about when he growed up, if I knowed why he was so diff'rent, never did fit in like ever'body else, couldn't ever adjust to nothin'. Even when he was a little bastard, I could tell he wasn't s'posed to be here. And now he comes along all these thirty-two years later and wants me to tell him why."

A strange chill crawled up L. D.'s spine. "Did you tell him somethin'?"

She laughed lowly. L. D. thought it seemed almost a cackle. "The truth," she growled. And suddenly those eyes were fixed on him, wild and wide and streaked with red. "I told him he'd have to go back to hell if he wanted to fit in. That's where he come from, you know, straight from hell. I heard it all right there in that other room when his grandfather's uncle died—ninety-nine, the old devil was. He told me how he got married when he was seventeen and watched her die havin' that baby just like my sister done, and the way just the two of them was left and how he hated that boy for it all. How one mornin' the kin found that boy of his dead in bed.

"Nobody could understand it, the way he died so sudden, just seven years old. They wrapped that boy in flour sacks and buried him out back, but the wolves and dogs dug him up and they never did find all of him again.

"Charlie was six the first time that old man ever laid eyes on him, and the old devil just went to shakin' and never did stop till he died that same night. I was right there with him and heard ever' last word. Huh! He'd took a pillow and smothered that boy of his to death back in the eighteen nineties and thought it was over and done with—till Charlie walked in. He took one look at him and knowed he hadn't done a good enough job, that that boy of his had come back, right out of his grave."

She cackled again. "Yeah, you look at me like I hadn't got good sense—just like I looked at that old man till he had me go through that drawer."

She took one last drag on the cigarette and ground the butt into the fruit jar lid. Standing, she crossed to a china cabinet to rummage through a drawer and return to L. D. Almost viciously, she shoved an old tintype into his lap.

"Here! Look at this boy! That black hair, that face, how he looks around the eyes!"

She could damned sure startle a person with those outbursts, thought L. D., taking the tintype to glance at the young boy straddling a wire chair and cupping a ball in his hands. "Yes, ma'am, I see."

"You don't see *nothin'*. Now look at this, look at this picture of Charlie took seventy-five years later when that other boy was long dead and buried!"

She plunged a small, framed photo into L. D.'s lap, only to have him look up at her apologetically. "Ma'am, I'm sorry I got you all so upset this way. I—"

"Look at it, damn you!"

He lowered his eyes to it, started, whirled to face her, then examined it carefully. His heart suddenly hammered and his throat went dry, and with fingers strangely sweaty and unsteady he slid the tintype out from under the framed photo and studied them side-by-side.

L. D. was no anthropologist, and maybe his eyes weren't trained for this sort of thing, but nevertheless as he impulsively stood and made his way into the light falling through the open doorway, he was stunned by the uncanny resemblance of the two youths. Identical twins could not have looked more alike—and yet one picture was of Charlie, and the other of a boy dead a hundred years.

"I . . ." L. D. swallowed hard and turned again to the woman. "You're tellin' me"—he glanced again at the photos—"this picture's the boy that got murdered way back there and this other one's Charlie?"

"I'm tellin' you just what I told *him*, that he don't have no bus'ness bein' here, that he belongs back in the eighteen hundreds, either there or in hell."

L. D. took a deep breath and studied the photos again, forcing himself to think rationally despite the bizarre suggestions planted in his mind. "Charlie and this other boy would've been kin, some kind of distant cousins—wouldn't they?" The question was more for himself than for the woman. "*That's* why there's a resemblance. Charlie's just a throwback."

She shoved them back in his hands. "Look at them, damn you! Don't you have eyes? Can't you see there ain't no two people in the world can look that much alike, especially when one of them's somebody that ever'body knows never did belong here?"

L. D. glanced at the photos again and his throat knotted up. "You told him that," he said quietly. "You told him and showed him these pictures, and now he thinks he really *does* belong back in the eighteen hundreds. You told him that and now he's out there just ridin' like hell—with no place to go."

Placing the portraits on the lamp table, L. D. found a deep breath and headed out the door into the warm night.

But an icy chill went with him, choking his throat every step.

* * *

As the tires sang all the way back out caliched Walnut Road, L. D. tried to absorb what he had just learned. Okay, so those two boys looked a lot alike, enough to chill him every time he thought about it. And that long-ago murder and the dug-up grave and the old man dying the first time he saw Charlie—none of it would have had any place in a sheriff's world, much less a cowboy's, except for one important aspect.

Damn it, wouldn't that explain Charlie once and for all? Why he'd always groped through life half-blind, an obvious misfit?

A sudden bump in the road jolted L. D., and he shook his head and half-laughed. *Boy*, he thought, *she sure filled my mind with it, didn't she?*

So *what* if they resembled one another—they were distantly related, and genetics could sure play tricks sometimes, even with himself. Wasn't Sarah always teasing him about those cat eyes of his, when no other family member had a trace of green except one grandparent?

Anyway, it didn't really matter what he thought. All that made any difference was what Charlie believed—and he believed for sure now that he was out-of-time, and that there wasn't a thing he could do about it except ride deeper into a place where time had stood still the past hundred years.

And L. D. had to find him before anyone else did.

Chapter Ten

L. D. could read the blood lust in their eyes the moment dawn broke on the cedared Divide.

At the end of passable road, they milled around the vehicles and trailers, taut-faced men as skittish as the horses tied to the bumpers. He studied them one at a time as he tightened the girth strap behind his animal's forelegs. Down along the gelding's nose he sighted Milton fumbling with a box of thirty-eight caliber shells, spilling more than he slipped inside his cartridge belt. Over the cantle of the saddle he saw Syers lean into a DPS car and come out clutching several Ruger clips. And past the horse's swishing tail he found Fowler, in the company of a Jim Ned deputy and state troopers, sighting-in his 30.06 over the supporting frame of an open pickup door.

They were ready to kill, but even though it was Charlie out there, L. D. understood. After all, just the night before, they had packed Powers' body back over this same road, and they believed him killed at Charlie's hands. Murder an average citizen and law enforcement officers looked upon apprehending the perpetrator as a job. But kill one of their own and they all took it personally, as though a one-on-one vendetta were in order, because it could have been any of them just as easily.

Satisfied with the girth strap, L. D. straightened and looked over his shoulder to see McBee approaching; the old rancher had been adjusting the saddles on the other horses. "Well," he told L. D., "I'm a-turnin' it over to you boys today, fresh horses and all. Durned ol' knees are botherin' me."

"Yes, sir. I was gonna ask you to stay in today. Just too dangerous out there. Anything we oughta know about that pasture 'fore we head out?"

The old man rubbed the side of his nose. "Well, I'll tell ya. Appears to me, that boy's a-headin' further away from the highway all the time. Far as we was in last night, he's still got thirty-five, forty miles of dat-blamed rough country left with ain't even a passable cow trail, much less a road, all the way till that railroad and blacktop jumps up. Nothin' much out there 'cept a bunch of big pastures, some goats, a sore-eyed old bull, and a few old outlaw horses." He nodded to the tarpaulin tied behind the saddle on L. D.'s horse. "See you got your bedroll. Figurin' on stayin' out?"

From behind came a low, caustic laugh. L. D. turned to see Syers already mounted on his bay. "Don't that horse of yours have enough lard to haul around already?" snapped the ranger.

L. D. felt himself tense throughout. "Lard's one thing," he said, nodding to the bay and then fixing his eyes on the man. "The stuff I scrape off my boot in the cow lot's somethin' else."

Syers flushed and his lips tightened. "You better get it straight in your head just what I said last night, Hankins," he growled. He patted a .223 Ruger that L. D. recognized as Powers' from the blood smearing the stock. "Don't you forget even for a second and get between me and that cowboy friend of yours. He's a cop-killing SOB."

"That's for a jury to decide," said L. D.

"Wouldn't hurt my feelings any," spoke up Fowler, "if we brought him back draped over a horse just like that boy was."

The Jim Ned County deputy beside him half-snickered. "Sure would save the taxpayers the expense of a trial."

"Yeah," added a state trooper, "or the governor the trouble of shooting him up with a needle."

L. D. glanced over to find Milton looking down and patting his revolver as he mumbled inaudibly. "You got somethin' you want to add, Milton?" he snapped.

The young deputy whirled to him like a kid caught in the cookie jar and stiffened at the icy glare. "N-no sir, L. D.," he stammered.

L. D. turned away with a wag of his head and exhaled in disgust, then lifted his eyes to the thickening cedars marking a canyon rim ahead. *It's like they all want to get a notch in their guns, Charlie—and they'll damn sure try to do it too, if they see you before me.*

They rode, and as badly as L. D. felt on his second day back on a horse, he knew Milton, Fowler, and Syers felt worse. He wondered if all the hair were worn off the insides of their thighs, as was his. Certainly, the way they gingerly carried themselves in the saddles told him how sore they were throughout their upper legs. Even L. D. had forgotten the extreme tenderness that the first day of roundup could levy on the backs of the thighs, especially where they neared the buttocks.

Nor had the sun played favorites. Like his own, their faces, necks, ears, and wrists were broiled to a rich scarlet. But L. D. had avoided the rawness he noted on the meaty part of Milton's thumb and alongside its joint, courtesy of the deputy's grip on the saddle horn in downgrades. And too, he had no reason to rub his tricep, as he caught Fowler doing in payment for a day of pushing against the horn to maintain balance along declines.

Milton and Fowler openly complained, and Syers did his part by cursing as he squirmed with every stride of his horse. L. D. suddenly found himself deriving an odd sense of pleasure in watching the ranger reach back to push down against the cantle and hike up a leg to ease the pressure. But maybe L. D.'s amusement was a little too obvious, for when Syers looked up and caught his stare, he quickly straightened and did his best to mask the grimaces.

All in all, they were a sorry lot, even the extra Jim Ned County deputy, who seemed about as sure of himself astride a horse as Milton had the day before. *Yeah, Charlie,* thought L. D., *you've got us in your world, and what's it gonna do to us today?*

The fact that Charlie, so far, had headed generally northward led them to pass up the canyon in which they had sighted him the evening before. Although L. D. hoped the day would wear on and diminish the party's kill-happy attitude, he could not question Fowler's argument that they could gain ground by keeping to the high country. Topographic maps showed the cowboy would have to continue crossing elevated necks of land to hold a northerly course, and if he did so, they might easily pick up his trail on the grassy flats. Charlie's only alternatives, L. D. knew, were either to hole up in a canyon and wait to be caught, or to spill out into the eastern breaks and risk well-patrolled ranch roads.

As the helicopter whirring low in the east momentarily became lost in the rising sun, they reached the gyp-water windmill for which they had been riding the evening before. L. D., in the lead, decided to play one of the few aces he held against the brewing bloodshed. He reined up in front of the others, holding up their horses, and slung an arm toward the stunted cedars marking a gully a quarter-mile away at a canyon head.

"Over yonder, where Powers got shot," he said. "There's been a man killed, and we hadn't even looked that scene over good yet."

"Oh hell," said Syers disgustedly.

"You still holding to that ricochet idea?" asked Fowler.

Syers breathed sharply. "Hell, he did his damndest yesterday to point out a broke-off outcrop and couldn't." And then to L. D., "It wouldn't mean a damn thing anyway if you did—that friend of yours was pouring all kinds of lead at our butts."

L. D. breathed sharply and glanced at Fowler and Milton before fixing his eyes on the ranger. "I counted *one* shot, Syers. How many did *y'all* count?" He inhaled deeply and looked again toward the gully. "We're a sorry bunch of investigators if we don't go look that thing over in the light of day."

"That gully's not going anywhere," snapped Syers. "There's time for that later. We've got a manhunt on our hands, if you haven't forgotten, *Sheriff*."

Fowler scanned the grassy tableland ahead. "I think Gene's right. Maybe he's a murderer and maybe not, but he's out there armed and dangerous and he's had all night to travel in. No telling how far behind we've fallen already. I'm for pushing ahead, trying to pick up his sign, unless you still want to be doing this next month. That crime scene can be fine-combed later."

Fowler's deputy backed him up with a nod.

"And when will that be, Ernest?" demanded L. D. "After maybe an innocent man's been murdered himself?"

Fowler just looked at him and shook his head. "I tried to tell you that you're too close to this, Sheriff, that you should pull yourself off of this."

Syers kicked his horse in the side. "Let's go get that SOB," he growled, brushing past L. D.'s roan and taking off through the tableland away from the gully.

Fowler glanced at L. D., then he and his deputy both turned their horses in pursuit of Syers. L. D. sat staring after them for long moments, frustrated and feeling all control fast slipping away.

"*I'll* go with you, L. D."

Turning, he saw Milton alone waiting beside him. L. D. glanced back toward the gully, then shook his head.

"Forget it, Milton," he said. Hell, he told himself, it wasn't his deputy he had to convince.

But as he took his animal after the other riders, he wondered if maybe the real reason he had passed up the chance was because he was afraid of finding out something he didn't want to know.

He hadn't ridden far until Milton called after him, and he looked around and slowed to allow the younger man to catch up. He read unvoiced words in Milton's face as he neared, but as they came abreast, the deputy lowered his eyes to ride in silence. Finally L. D. heard him sigh deeply.

"About yesterday, L. D.," the younger man said quietly, without raising his head.

"You've already talked to me about yesterday, Milton," L. D. said impatiently.

The younger man stammered around for a moment, still avoiding eye contact. "You know me, L. D.; sometimes my mouth just gets to working faster than my head."

"Yeah."

Only now did Milton look up. "I-I've been working with you for over two years now, and I know if you pass up some kind of clue, you either don't see it or you've got a real good reason to. I . . . I just want you to know that you can count on me from here on out."

"Well, then, Milton, first thing I'll count on you doin' is keepin' that thirty-eight where it is."

Milton looked down at his holstered revolver and then back at L. D. with a quizzical expression.

"We're not out here to go killin' nobody," L. D. went on. "We're out here to bring Charlie Lyles back in alive so he can do some more time on that parole violation and be tried for stealin' that horse. There's nobody been charged with murder—but if we keep pushin' him to where he thinks he hadn't got a choice, there's damned sure *liable* to be some more killin'."

"But the justice of the peace said he was probably going to rule homicide."

"He's not rulin' *anything* till he gets that autopsy and ballistics report back. If he does rule murder, well, that's one thing, but till then we've got to all keep our cool."

Especially you, Charlie, he thought. *Especially a cowboy who just can't ride out of all these modern times no matter how hard he tries.*

"You can count on me, L. D.," repeated Milton.

Can I? thought L. D., turning away. *Can I really?*

With Fowler laying a course with topographic map and compass, they rode northwest through grassland sentineled by occasional big mesquites and stands of prickly pear that rose breast-high on the horses. In doing so, they bypassed four more inlet canyons, all deep and narrow, before finally veering into the mid-morning sun and onto a broad flat thrusting reef-like over the breaks. They angled across to the almost impenetrable brush hugging the south rim, then scouted the less-timbered zone alongside, where the green of cedars contrasted with clearings of flagstone and gray spear grass.

In late morning they picked up his trail, northbound and unmistakable, and the chase was on through orange-blooming cacti that branded the rocky tableland. While Syers fell back to radio for aerial reconnaissance, L. D. loped his roan on up to a dead mesquite that stood monument-like against a grassy flat dotted with scrub cedar. There, he dismounted and knelt with reins in hand to find flies buzzing around fetid horse droppings still warm to the touch.

Good Lord, Charlie, he cried silently, lifting his eyes to the veldt ahead, *you've gone and let us catch up. You've gone and left your trail plain enough so ever'body can see, and now we've caught you. Don't you know they're goin' to kill you?*

"It's fresh, L. D.—that horse has just been here."

He looked around to see Milton reining up alongside the roan.

"Yeah."

He quickly mounted and, ignoring Milton's further comments, spurred his horse into a gallop down Charlie's trail. *I'm comin' after you, Charlie!* he cried silently, riding on the balls of his feet as he leaned in against the roan's neck. He could feel the gelding's heartbeat through his legs and hear its pants as the hooves pounded out a primitive drumbeat. *I'm ridin' you down before they go and kill you!*

He far-outdistanced the other men, the terrain past the gelding's head bursting upon him in bounding flashes of color: the yellow of scorched grassland, the green of scattered cedars, the bleach-white of coyote bones, the red of prickly pear blooms and the purple of filaree. His horse shied at a sudden jackrabbit, and again at the choppy whir of the helicopter passing over. He pushed the animal hard for a minute more, its hindquarters foaming as it reached out again and again with its lanky forelegs for the shadow that always glided just in front.

Then he plunged through a mott of Christmas tree-like cedars and passed a last massive clump to explode upon a net wire fence that set his snorting horse planting its feet and plowing through the ground. L. D. didn't have time even to think about stepping off; inertia threw him right over the gelding's downed head and hard against the base of the fence.

Back behind the last shielding cedars, the others found him, aching and red-faced, when they came leading his horse up.

"Try staying on your damned horse," growled Syers.

"Go to hell," snapped L. D., angrily snatching the reins of the roan from Milton.

"We're on his tail," Fowler said excitedly. "They saw him from the air, right ahead of you. They caught a glimpse of him riding into the timber. What's past these trees?"

L. D. planted a boot in the stirrup. "A fence," he said disgustedly, swinging up. "Past that's a clearing, maybe fifty yards, then heavy brush."

Syers turned his horse back into a small clearing and reached for the radio as he waved an arm to the helicopter hovering ahead. "Get a fix on me, back to your south," he ordered. "I want to know where he is from us, the lay of the land."

Through overhanging brush L. D. watched the chopper's tail swing away as it turned. He couldn't distinguish the pilot's response, but Syers, upon returning to the cedar clump, repeated it.

"We've got the SOB," he growled. He nodded past the big cedars. "Other side of that clearing's a stretch of heavy timber about a hundred yards wide and eighty yards deep, leading right up to steep rimrock falling away. They watched him go in and he didn't come out. We're going in there and flush him out—damn, where's a good body bag when you need one?" He half-laughed.

"We better post somebody on each side of it," said Fowler, whose back was half-turned to L. D. though their horses were side-by-side. "Get that chopper to guard the back rim. That'll leave three of us to go in and shake him out—if he hits one of those clearings, we can open up. We better start by spraying that line of brush—it'd be just like him to be laying in wait there, ready to blow a hole through the first thing that walks out in the open."

L. D. reached out to clutch Fowler's shoulder and spin him around. "The hell we will! Aren't you forgettin' somethin', Ernest? That you don't go shootin' a man for just stealin' a horse?"

Fowler's hawk-like face flushed. "Just back off, Sheriff," he angrily challenged. "Just back off right now."

Syers laughed quietly as he lowered the radio after relaying orders to the helicopter crew. "I don't know, Fowler, maybe he's right. That SOB's out there playing cowboys and Indians, and they damned sure didn't shoot a horse thief back in those days. They hung him."

L. D. breathed sharply. "If he's in there, I want the chance to go in after him, just me. I want the chance to talk to him face-to-face, see if I can't get him to come on back in with me."

"You're a damn fool, Hankins," snapped Syers.

"He knows me. I can talk to him, tell him some things, get him to forget this whole thing and come on back."

Fowler shook his head in disgust. "You *are* a fool if you think Lyles has got the same kind of loyalty to you that you've got for him. Your trouble is, you can't look at him as a fugitive, just as a friend. Well, I've been on the other side of it. I *know* him for what he is when the law gets after him. I watched him spin that jeep around and drive like hell when he saw us coming—and that was just for assault and auto theft, not for maybe shooting and killing a Texas Ranger."

"What skin is it off *your* nose, anyway, Ernest?" dep anded L. D. "I go in, bring him out, it saves ever'body a lot of trouble. I don't come back, well, it hasn't done anything but delay y'all's plan a couple of minutes. I'm goin' on in—by myself."

Syers' cheek twitched. "I wouldn't trust you any farther that I can throw that damned horse of yours."

"Ride out in that clearing," warned Fowler, "and he can pick you off like a tin can on a fence."

"Not Charlie. Not to me." He turned his horse toward the shielding clump of cedars.

"You better use some common sense and stay where you are," urged Fowler.

"Maybe you oughta not do it, L. D.," said Milton. "He might've been your friend one time, but he's gone kill-crazy now."

"I'm goin', Milton."

"Oh hell," sighed Syers, "if he's that anxious to get his head blowed off, let the idiot go. Fowler, go ahead and circle your deputy around there on the east side of that thicket and Hankins' deputy here can cover the west. I'll have the chopper guarding the back door—you know, just in case Hankins here forgets whose side he's on again and tries to find a way out for that SOB."

L. D.'s eyes narrowed as he glared at the ranger, but now wasn't the time for further altercation. Instead, he nodded to Milton and the Jim Ned County deputy. "Milton, Deputy, y'all go ahead and take some wire cutters each and get started. Circle wide before you cut through so he don't see you and get spooked. I'll give y'all three minutes, then I'm startin' in."

They started away, and he checked his wristwatch and became oblivious to all else except that second hand inexorably ticking away the seconds of his life. It was taking them, one at a time, choking by degrees the last of those lofty dreams he had been too afraid to chase. And now, he was about to snuff out those same dreams for someone who'd had the courage, someone who'd never had a choice.

Two fifty-eight, two fifty-nine, three minutes. Reining his horse around the last guarding cedars, he glanced down the fence at the dangling wires Charlie had snipped, and then faced the broad clearing and thicket beyond.

"Charlie!" he yelled over the choppy whir of the helicopter. "Charlie Lyles! It's me! L. D.! I'm comin' in, just me, and I'm not gonna be holdin' a gun! You hear me, Charlie? I'm comin' in!"

And as he took a deep breath and turned his roan down the fence and through the breach, he thought about Sarah trying to go on alone while he lay dead in his own blood in that grassy flat.

Chapter Eleven

The crisp snap of a twig ahead brought L. D. jerking the
roan's head back at the timber's edge.

Good God, Charlie, he silently cried, staring hard through
berried shrubs, red shimmering against green. *I'm stakin' my
life on you still bein' what I think you are, on you not turnin'
that rifle on me.*

He found a deep breath, remembering how together they
once had cut outlaw steers out of the JA thickets.

"Charlie?" he called with deliberate calmness. "Charlie,
I'm comin' in to talk."

He swallowed hard and urged his horse on into the timber.
He brushed past a thick cedar alive with the buzz of cicadas,
and a dead limb rasping across his hat all but drowned-out
the musical sound of an overturned pebble rolling along
base rock ahead.

Again, he froze.

*Lord, Charlie. It's not some gun-crazy greenhorn out
here—it's me, stickin' my neck out for you.*

He went on, feeling the tug of catclaw against his leggings
and tasting the sun-baked cedar, then stiffened at a sudden
movement through the greenery. Something was there, not
twenty yards ahead, stirring the cedars and thick undergrowth like a rushing wind.

*Are you fixin' to shoot me, Charlie? Good God, Charlie,
are you fixin' to shoot me?*

But the thrashing of limbs swept on from right to left, picking up speed to the drumming of hooves against rock.

He was making a run for it! He'd gone and gotten spooked and now he'd touched spurs to that horse and was riding like hell straight for Milton and a waiting gun!

"No!"

L. D.'s cry died in the whipping of brush and choppy drone of the helicopter, then he was reining his horse around and pushing hard back toward the clearing. Milton would panic! Charlie would explode out of the thicket right into his face and Milton would panic and pull that thirty-eight! He'd force Charlie to use that rifle, and if L. D. didn't reach the scene first by avoiding the timber, somebody would get killed!

Above the drum roll of hooves against turf he heard Milton yelling from off to his right, and when L. D. finally burst into the clearing to turn the roan down the line of brush, he saw Syers and Fowler well ahead and riding hard for the deputy. Spurring the roan into a gallop, L. D. quickly made up ground. But the thicket stretched only fifty yards before him, and the two men already were disappearing into the break where Milton kept sentry when there came the quick *boom! boom! boom!* of a revolver.

No!

No, Milton, damn you!

He wheeled his horse up the park-like zone just in time to see three geldings spook at a sudden fusillade from their riders. Milton's extended arms recoiled three times in quick succession from blasts from his thirty-eight; Fowler rocked back in the saddle with each boom of the 30.06; Syers careened to the quick spray of thirty .223 rounds that cut a brushy cedar in half. And then three snorting horses had downed their heads and begun running and pitching wildly, throwing Milton hard to his shoulder, brushing Fowler against a limb that peeled him backwards from the saddle, spilling Syers on his buttocks in fresh horse manure.

L. D.'s horse, too, shied at the gunfire, but he weathered the jumps and spurred the animal under control as he whirled wide-eyed and afraid at the thicket. Just inside, cedar needles and scrub oak leaves fluttered down like snow.

"Kill the bastard! Kill the bastard!" cried Milton, frantically coming to a crouch to snap the firing pin of his revolver time and again against spent cartridges.

Reining up his horse alongside him, L. D. slipped his foot free of the stirrup and viciously kicked the revolver from his hand. "Damn it, Milton, that's enough!" he cried. "Can't you tell you don't have any more damned bullets?"

"I cut that SOB in half!" Syers was yelling, rubbing his cheek into his shoulder and leaving his shirt smeared with manure. He stood popping another clip into his Ruger to face the thicket.

"We got him! I know we got him!" Fowler shouted, pawing at a red-streaked cut at his brow and running over to retrieve his 30.06. "I saw him fall! He went down before he even got a shot off! I told you he'd hang himself if we gave him rope enough!"

"He-he was coming right at me," Milton was babbling excitedly. "He-he was bearing down right on me and I knew I had to get him, knew I had to lower the boom on him right then and there."

L. D. shuddered, fear enveloping him like a dark, heavy shadow as he turned the roan into the thicket. *Good God, Charlie, they've killed you! Good God, Charlie, they've killed you!*

Beyond the shielding foliage he burst breathless, ashen, and chilled upon the grisly scene—and a few seconds later he turned to stare in disbelief at the smug features of Syers and Fowler, who had rushed after him on foot so as not to miss out on the thrill of the kill.

Shaken and outraged, L. D. swallowed hard, remembering the cowboy, and found a deep breath. "Nice work, Syers, Ernest," he snapped caustically, slinging his head back

behind him. "Y'all just had to do it, didn't you? Y'all just
had to go shootin' crazy as hell at an outlaw, and the only
damned thing you can hit's one of McBee's old swaybacked
outlaw horses."

The moment Charlie looked up through limbs to see the
helicopter's bubble dip and the tail swing toward him, he
spurred his horse out onto the rimrock and over the edge.

They went crashing down through scrub cedars and two
more ledges of rock, the horse sitting back to plow with stiff
forelegs that became fluid in quick, regular lunges. Even
above the animal's snorting and the rumble of scree falling
away from hooves, Charlie could still hear the helicopter's
rotors. He reached the towering cedars hugging the lower
slope and checked over his shoulder to find only patterned
sky through the limbs, then he pushed the animal hard on
down to the narrow canyon floor.

He had sensed L. D. would intensify the hunt today; the
gunfire of the evening before, even though he hadn't understood it, had told him as much. It had driven him to press on
through much of the night, where terrain and undergrowth
had allowed, and even to risk open tableland by daylight. In
canyon bottoms he had backtracked and circled to confuse
his trackers, yet surprisingly they had narrowed the gap.
Even now, he couldn't tarry—he knew that this gulch below
the timbered flat would be the next place they would comb.

He turned the gelding up the opposite cedared slope and
felt the strength wrenched from the animal with every stride
as it struggled with his weight and that of the saddle. He realized his two hundred thirty pounds would test even a fresh,
grain-fed horse on a morning roundup through such rough
country, much less an animal denied anything but grass and
pushed relentlessly for almost two days now.

Where timber opened up to rimrock he held the gelding
long enough to look back and find the helicopter; it hovered

over the rim behind, its bubble turned away. Then he took the horse on up through a break in the rimrock and into the scrub oak and cedars on the summit.

He wheeled the animal at a sudden fusillade that reverberated through the gulch. Through wind-blown briars and screeching limbs he looked across-canyon to see three riders wildly shooting into the thicket greenery, spooking their own horses, and a fourth horseman bursting into view. Charlie recognized L. D. in an instant, just as he recognized three strong, grain-fed horses burying heads between forelegs and unceremoniously throwing novice riders to the ground.

Regular rodeo, L. D., he thought. *That tenderfoot outfit wouldn't know how to climb in and shut the door even if you saddled 'em up on those ol' form-fitters.*

He continued to study the scene intently as L. D. reined up his horse before one of the downed men and viciously kicked a pistol from his hand. Strangely, Charlie felt suddenly reassured; L. D., at least, retained a little common sense. But the others . . .

He breathed deeply and shook his head. *Looks like they all got a pretty good case of loco, L. D. What the hell you lettin' 'em go shootin' at me for, anyhow? I know I ain't a damned bit meaner than I was in that line camp with you.*

But what Charlie *didn't* know was how long he could outdistance even greenhorns astride fresh horses when his own animal was weakening by the moment. One thing was certain though—now that he had found his own world, he was not about to relinquish it.

Watching the riderless horses go running away, pitching to the wildly flying stirrups that flopped hard against backs and sides, Charlie formulated a plan to fight back. He had no way of knowing that already one man was dead and another hospitalized, but it was apparent that the riders across-canyon probably couldn't endure a war of attrition for long. They were novices to the backcountry, except for L. D., and he obviously had let himself grow soft. Somehow, Charlie had to force them to give up the chase before his own horse wore down.

I'm leadin' y'all on a ride you'll never forget, he called silently across the gulch. He glanced at his spur rowels, rattling in a sudden gust. *I'm hangin' 'em in to you so bad it'll knock the hair off of you. I'm leadin' you deeper into my country, L. D., and I'm gonna push y'all so hard it'll break y'all's will, a little bit at a time. And if that don't work—hell, I don't want to hafta shoot nobody, 'less they make me. And damn it, L. D., you're pretty close to makin' me.*

Bending over, he snapped a couple of dead limbs in a cedar and then turned his horse and spurred it away from the brushy rim.

Down into steaming canyons tangled with underbrush and up through stunted cedars twisting out of rimrock, L. D. walked under a broiling afternoon sun and led his horse. Even on canyon floors and mesa grasslands where he could safely ride and avoid the heaving lungs of a man-gone-soft, he did so in silence, directing the other men purely by example. Hell, he was so damned mad at himself that talking was the last thing he wanted to do.

He couldn't even muster any anger toward Milton—who trailed along behind with lowered eyes—only something akin to pity. After all, L. D. had only himself to blame for hiring the deputy, and he guessed he'd been a damned poor judge of character in that respect. And what about Syers bearing down with that semi-automatic like it was the opening minute of deer season, or Fowler following suit? Or Powers being dissected at that pathology lab or that deputy lying up in that hospital? L. D. alone had asked for their help, and in return he had gotten inexperience and irresponsibility, a dead man and an injured one. He had turned a parole violator and horse thief into a cop killer, and now he just didn't know where it was all going to end. Why the hell couldn't he just have borrowed a horse off old man McBee and taken off after Charlie on his own?

At least, the episode in the mesa thicket had served to subdue the others, that and the rigors of the trail. They were a morose and sullen bunch trudging stiff-legged with reins in hands down steep slopes and struggling weak-kneed up steeper ones, or bouncing along grimacing with every stride of their horses on canyon or high country flats. If they spoke at all, it was only in impatient barks punctuated by curses, but there were enough epithets still directed at Charlie to make L. D. wonder if their blood lust had been curbed or just honed to a fine edge.

You're a leg up on us again, Charlie, he thought, lifting his eyes toward the greenery of a bluff that hid north. *Sure missed a helluva sight, us chasin' those boogered horses across that flat. Now, ever'body's got some time to think, feel that sun beatin' down, all those saddle sores. It's either gonna chase 'em back in or start things to festerin' and make it all worse.*

For L. D.'s part, he had never felt so horsewhipped by saddle stock travel in his life. He squinted through those blue-tinted driving shades Sarah had given him and didn't know whether to dread most the inevitable canyon slopes that demanded trudging on aching knees, or the succeeding flats where stabbing pains in his raw thighs signaled every stride of his horse. All he did know was that he was damned mad at Sarah for not chewing him out whenever he'd reached for all those second helpings over the years. And even madder at himself for trying to blame it on her.

The relentless miles drew on under a cloudless sky that cooked lips and streamed sweat down broiled necks. Ever so often, L. D. would sip from his canteen or lift his hat to dampen the crook of his arm with his head and catch the wind, but those were momentary respites from conditions ideal for heat exhaustion or stroke. In mid afternoon he found himself astride the roan and nodding along in concert with the animal, his eyes dully taking in the harmonious way the horse walking before him lifted a forefoot just in time for the trailing hoof to drop neatly into the just-formed track. He snapped into full awareness only when the Jim Ned County deputy astride that animal stopped and plucked a bit of cloth from a thorn marking the fringe of a tableland mesquite thicket.

"Caught him in the shoulder," said the deputy, holding it aloft to wave in the wind. He nodded past the first thorny clump to the dead limbs clawing out of lacy-leafed greenery. "Went right on through there."

L. D., second in line, frowned and glanced around. "Hang on a minute, deputy. We've kinda veered off to one side here, got in some stuff he wouldn't normally take a horse through. All those thorns'll have a horse's breast bleedin' like you took a knife to him." He leaned over to study the ground. "These your tracks or his, or are you steppin' on 'em?"

"Look, there's more on that limb up there."

Before L. D. even sighted the tatter clinging to a thorn and rippling in the wind, the deputy already had urged his horse inside the thicket. Limbs scratched across his chaps and strafed his arms. "Things'll eat you alive," commented the deputy, proceeding slowly in order to sweep back the limber branches left unparted by the animal's torso.

Still, L. D. held his horse. *You wouldn't've done this, Charlie*, he said silently, noting how the thicket thinned left and right, hinting at easier passage on its perimeter. *You wouldn't've took a horse through there and cut him all up when you could've rode around.*

"What the hell you waiting on, Hankins?" snapped Syers, suddenly alongside.

A loud snorting and the rattle of a saddle turned them both to the brush, where the deputy's horse suddenly shied at a quick movement at its feet and bolted deeper into the thicket. The man yelled and ducked, losing all control of the animal as he tried to fend off the barbed limbs that slapped viciously at his shoulders and thighs.

"Hold that horse!" cried L. D., taking the roan after him.

He pulled his hat down low on his brow and held it there, protecting his eyes from the thrashing brush. Ten yards inside, his horse dodged, having scared up the same jackrabbit that had spooked the deputy's animal. Through leafy, pliant limbs and crisp dead ones he went crashing on, whipped like a gassy cowboy convicted of campfire impropriety and run through a kangaroo court leggings line. But this time, one- and two-inch thorns punctuated each blow, and there was no raucous laughter accompanying it.

"Get that horse stopped—pull back on the reins!" yelled L. D., finding the animal still a blur through greenery ahead.

His roan carried him recklessly through catclaw and thickening mesquites, then suddenly a powerful and flexible limb—left spring-loaded by the horse's forward momentum—catapulted back to drive a thorn hard through his leggings and into his knee.

He cried out to paralyzing pain that exploded needle-like through his lower leg. Instantly sickened throughout by the shock, he quickly reined up his horse to double over wincing and clutching at his knee, where a heavy thorn lay imbedded in the badly worn leather of his chaps.

Damn! He'd gone and paid the price for trusting leggings so worn and thin, for letting the too-supple leather stretch so tightly over his knee.

"I'm crippled!" he yelled back to the officers outside the thicket. "Somebody else gotta help that deputy!"

But the deputy already had stopped his horse, to his own low moaning, and it wasn't until after both riders had picked their way out of the brush that L. D. realized the deputy's own injuries. Of course, his shirt sleeves were ripped and his arms bleeding, as were L. D.'s, and his cheek and neck bore ugly scratches, but it was the arm he carried folded across his chest that evoked agony in his face as he slowly rocked to visceral groans.

"What the hell's the matter with him?" asked Syers.

"Got a damned thorn sticking clean through his wrist!" exclaimed Fowler, dismounting to assist the man off his horse.

L. D. saw it too—a two-inch thorn completely piercing a bleeding wrist—but he was having troubles of his own in dismounting with a hurt left knee. He succeeded only by slipping his left boot out of the stirrup and leaning into the saddle horn to slide off on his stomach. Wincing as he tried to bear weight, he wrenched a broken thorn from the chaps before removing them and finding a puncture wound just below the base of his kneecap.

"You all right, L. D.?" asked a restrained Milton, suddenly at his side.

He found his deputy's eyes. Milton lowered them. "Damned near crippled me," said L. D. He turned to Fowler, who was with the shaken officer. "He all right?"

Fowler glanced around; he stood leaned over the man's arm, supporting and tending it. "Got it pulled out, but the hull stayed in."

"Yeah, that'll happen," said L. D., gingerly testing his knee and studying the ground at the thicket's fringe. He looked up. "Deputy, you gonna be able to make it?"

The man found a deep breath and swallowed hard. "I don't know," he said, wincing. "Kills me . . . to try to . . . close my hand."

"Oh, hell," said Syers impatiently. "Just give him some aspirin and let's get after that cowboy. Bastard's about at the end of his rope right now if he runs like a scared rabbit through thorns like *that*."

L. D. whirled to Syers. "The hell he is!" he snapped, all the pain finding an outlet in anger. He slung his arm to the turf and then swept it across the greenery before them. "You think he went through there? Look at those horses—see how they're all bleedin' in the breast and shoulders? Charlie wouldn't *do* that to his horse—and he didn't mean it to happen to ours—just to us."

"You saying Lyles didn't go through there?" asked Fowler. "When those thorns caught him so bad in the arm it tore some of his shirt off?"

"Looka here, Ernest—see all the ground there, way that grass is layin'? It's been pulled up, laid over. Come here, take a look, here, there, over yonder, leadin' clean around those trees. It's coverin' up Charlie Lyles' horse tracks. He planned it so we'd come along here and see those rags hangin' there and run smack-dab through those mesquites— just like the greenhorn bunch we are."

And as they mounted up to ride on, L. D. couldn't decide if the feeling suddenly surging through him was dismay or admiration.

Chapter Twelve

L. D.'s knee ached to the jostling gait of the roan as they trailed the cowboy on across the plateau. He had never caught a thorn in a joint before, and he thought he already could feel it swelling through his chaps. Damn, it hurt, but he knew it was nothing compared to the agony of the deputy, who rode grimacing and moaning as he clutched his forearm to his chest. It was the worst thorn wound L. D. had ever seen, and he couldn't help thinking about the JAs and how old cowboy Tom had told Charlie and him about a long-ago vaquero taking a mesquite thorn in the finger and dying of blood poisoning.

As the afternoon wore on, matters grew only worse. The sun was like a fire as Charlie's trail led them across grassy flats barren of shade except for skeletons of dead mesquites. L. D. watched the riders about him unconsciously slow the pace to a crawl and then bounce along almost in a daze. L. D. remembered the June sun from his days on the JAs and knew it for the killer it was. He read it in the broiled faces and scarlet necks, the cracked lips and glazed eyes. He felt it in his throat, a creeping dryness such as a cowboy knows in riding drag through a haze of dust. An excruciating cramp that brought him clutching his calf told him of salt depletion through sweat, and a slight fever and dizziness reminded him of his own intensifying sunburn.

At one point, the whir of the helicopter brought him lifting his eyes to find it eclipsing the sun. Tiredly, he wondered why Charlie would have risked such an exposed area in daylight—unless Syers had been right. Maybe he *was* feeling the squeeze chute closing in. But was he really desperate to get away, or just anxious to face them again somehow down the trail?

For a long while the dehydrating sun seemed suspended in the sky. Then the ground turned rocky, and the tonal change in the hoofbeats roused L. D. and he saw that the shadow of horse and rider extended long at his side. In a stretch of tasajillo and prickly pear the flats began to sink almost imperceptibly, until Charlie's trail led them through crowding cedars which the gusting wind stirred like milling cattle.

With the helicopter providing advance surveillance, they picked their way through the brush to burst upon whitewashed rimrock picketed by dead cedars and falling away in stages. A stiff wind blew up out of a broad canyon, and L. D. was not alone in lifting his hat to cool his sweat.

Fowler steadied his horse at the rim and peered over the edge; it dropped thirty vertical feet to a narrow shelf. "Nobody went off *that*," he commented. He studied the rimrock left and right, finding it curving out of sight behind jutting outcrops and twisted cedars. "So which way did he go?"

"Hell, I don't know," said Syers impatiently. "Damned chopper can't help us any either. It's enough to drive a man back to a cold six-pack and that little redhead at the cafe."

Milton shifted in the saddle to the creak of leather and rubbed the back of his thigh. "If I ever even *see* a horse after all this, I'm running the other way."

"Never saw a sun that'd bake your brains the way this one does," said Fowler, glancing up at it.

L. D. seized the moment.

"Maybe it's time you men all started back in. Look at how the sun's cooked y'all, the way that boy's sufferin' with that thorn, how those horses are all foamed up. Right now, it's gonna be a long hard ride to make it back in 'fore dark, and ever' step you take the other way is one more you gotta make to get back."

"You talk like you're not going with us," said Fowler, studying him cynically.

Syers sneered. "Why, he's got his bedroll, Fowler," he snapped sarcastically. "Maybe he's gonna make a pallet for himself and that bastard friend of his tonight."

The remark sent a wave of pain through L. D.'s knee like the twist of a knife. He inhaled deeply and shook his head. "Guess it gets tiresome, don't it, Syers, your mother runnin' out from under the porch that a-way and bitin' you in the ankle ever' time you get home."

Syers flushed, but it was L. D. who went on. "Now I got up this manhunt to go out after Charlie Lyles, and that's just what I'm gonna do—go out after him. Y'all are not used to this—me neither *now*. But I've spent enough nights out to know how to get some rest, while y'all will just toss and turn on a bunch of hard rocks and be beat up twice as bad come mornin'."

Syers cursed and glanced at the others. "He's sitting over there, going on about what bad shape everybody's in, when he's in worse shape than *anybody*. Couldn't even get off his damned horse back at those mesquites." He turned to sneer at L. D. "Finally, got your chance to play big-shot and order everybody around, didn't you, Hankins? A few hundred people mark your name down on a piece of paper and now you're a big lawman. Why, even your own deputy there's a helluva lot more qualified than you are—at least he got certified as a public peace officer, and what was it you did before they elected you? You drove a truck full of stinking sheep, while I was getting a degree in investigative techniques and going through DPS boot camp and putting in all those years working my way up to the Rangers. Sixteen, seventeen different law officers in the state, and you sheriffs are the only ones that don't even have to get certified. Yeah, go ahead and tell us about the two kinds of training you *have* had—little, and damned little."

L. D. swept his arm in an arc across the plummeting canyon. "Look around you, Syers—did they train you for *this*? Yeah, maybe in some big city all those degrees and investigative techniques will do you some good, but out here I stand a better chance of catchin' him than any of y'all, 'cause I know him."

Syers' cheek twitched. "I wouldn't any more trust you out here alone with that cop killer than I could carry your fat rear up that cliff."

"While we're here yappin' at each other," said L. D., "Charlie's stretchin' out the distance between him and us. If y'all are too stubborn to head back in, fine, and if nobody wants to follow my lead, well, that suits me for damned sure too. But I'm lettin' this horse carry my fat what-ever on down the rim, see what I can find. Somebody else oughta do the same the other way."

Without waiting for a response, he turned the roan down-rim and didn't know how to feel when he found Milton preceding him.

The two of them rode in silence to the rush of the updrafting wind and the strike of hoof against shelf. The sun's searing heat bore down on L. D.'s back and radiated up from the table rock, and his eyes fell on the foamy hindquarters of the leading bay and a part of him seemed to drift away, leaving only a dull awareness of the roan's head nodding endlessly before him. He asked himself where he was and where he was going, and no sooner did he realize, than his consciousness again took a half-step out of his body and the same questions haunted him.

At the nicker of his horse he shook himself into alertness and looked to his right to find a bouldered rise beginning to swell along the rimrock's mesa side. Already shoulder-high on his horse, and stair-stepping upward, it hovered over the doglegged rim all the way to a jutting point twenty yards away. There, it stood against the sky, a formidable face marked by a twisted cedar projecting out of solid rock two-thirds of the way up. The rimrock, meanwhile, continued unbroken, the canyon below yawning ever-deeper.

Holding up his horse, he glanced back up-rim and pondered whether the severe exposure at the cedar-tree point might have turned Charlie up the swelling rise while a horse still could have managed it. He looked at Milton, who still proceeded as thoughtlessly as ever, and exhaled impatiently.

"Maybe you oughta hold up a minute, Milton. Don't look to me much like a place Charlie would've gone. Sure gettin' narrow, too."

Milton reined up his horse and, half-turning, caught L. D.'s eyes and instantly lowered his own. "But . . . that point over there, L. D.," he whined. "He might've gone down, right on the other side. Hadn't . . . hadn't I ought to go check it out?"

L. D. breathed sharply; he was sick and tired of playing nursemaid. "Hell, Milton, you do what you want to," he snapped, turning the roan back up-rim.

At the first break in the rocky rise, L. D. stopped to study the rubbly game trail angling up between a pair of stunted cedars. The gusting wind thrashed the underlying catclaw, and for an instant L. D. thought he glimpsed a strand of horsehair glistening among the tiny green leaves. As loathe as his knee was to the idea, he went ahead and awkwardly dismounted, wincing and groaning. He had begun hobbling up the incline when the repeated snorting of Milton's horse turned him toward the jutting point, where, underscored by the roan's backbone, Milton and the bay stood against the rock bluff.

"Milton, you better watch that ledge!" L. D. shouted testily.

"I see something, L. D., on around the point here! Looks like a leather strap laying on the rim!"

L. D. watched him brashly proceed, ignoring his warning, and as rider and horse began to disappear around the palisade, L. D. turned away with an irritated wag of his head. He had just parted the catclaw to find a few clinging strands of horsehair when the loud and desperate snorting of Milton's horse again brought him whirling. The outcrop hid all but the gelding's hindquarters, but L. D. could tell immediately that the animal reared out-of-control on the brink of the drop-off.

"Damn it, Milton, get that horse under control!" he shouted.

"He's spooked!" Milton cried in panic. "The ledge's got too narrow around here!"

"If you can't turn him around or get him backed up, then climb off! That thing must drop eighty feet over there!"

"I can't, L. D.! Got a damned cliff in my shoulder!"

Damn! L. D. cried silently. *Why the hell wouldn't he listen to me?*

His thoughts ran wild as he hobbled down to dig a boot into his stirrup and painfully drag himself up across the roan. Milton and the bay would plummet into the canyon unless L. D. somehow seized that bridle—but how the hell could he even get close to it when the bay itself blocked the narrow ledge?

Good God, what would you *do, Charlie? If we was ridin' the Palo Duro rim and it was me out there, what would* you *do?*

Wheeling the roan about, he gigged it with his spurs up the pebbly game trail. The animal's power carried him up through catclaws and stunted cedars to the flagstone ridge rising right-to-left. There, he turned the animal up the incline and pushed hard for the crest, the gelding sloughing off uplifting shelves of rock with every stride.

Below and away, he could hear Milton's panicky cries and the frantic neighing of the bay, and even as he burst upon the crag's wind-swept summit, L. D. was spilling awkwardly from the saddle. His knee gave way to excruciating pain, leaving him scrambling like a three-legged dog over loose flagstone to throw himself prone and hang his head over cliff's edge.

Through the twisted limbs of the cedar jutting out of sheer rock two arm-lengths away, he could see Milton and the bay locked into a life-or-death struggle twenty feet below on a hollow-sounding ledge so narrow that the animal repeatedly reared and fought for footing. A forefoot would come down to slip over the edge, listing Milton precariously toward the canyon that dropped away dramatically, seventy-five feet to another rock shelf. Then the bay frantically would right itself, only to slam Milton hard against the wall and throw itself off-balance again.

"Hang on, Milton! I'm comin' down after you!" cried L. D.

Coming painfully to his knees, he pivoted on the edge and slipped a leg off sideways, searching for the gnarled base of the cedar that stayed just beyond his outstretched boot. Serrated rocks gnawed his forearm as his desperation grew with the increasingly frenzied thrashing of horse and rider below. He sighted-in the cedar one last time before twisting on his hip to flatten himself face-down on the bed-rock and slide both legs together over the precipice. His fingers clawed against limestone as his fleshy midriff grated across the jagged brim, and with feverish cries he groped blindly for the tree. He hoped to hell it was firmly rooted, and he wondered what Sarah would have thought about him dangling over a cliff with nothing but that lone scrub cedar between him and a damned long sleep.

He slipped a slick-soled boot down alongside hairy bark, then found it with his stronger leg. The bole complained and gave a little, petrifying him, and he drove his cheek into the cliff's edge and clamped his forearms tightly across the crowning bedrock. Grimacing and grunting, he clung there, staring down through uprushing wind and praying to God the cedar held. It did, even under his full weight, and with regained nerve he stretched out a hand for a gnarled upper branch, dropped in a half-turn, and seized it.

Through wind-thrashed greenery with biting spires and over jags of broken limbs, he fought his way out a couple of feet to a bough overhanging the frightened horse and rider. Rubble at the root system went tumbling down the cliff, and the limb creaked and sagged threateningly as L. D. hooked a leg over it and rolled clumsily underneath. He clung there like a fat possum, one arm crooked over the bark and the other stretched down toward the deputy, who somehow stayed astride the horse pawing at the sky.

"You gotta reach for me, Milton!" he cried above the bay's neighing.

Off-balance as the gelding stood upright, Milton could only hold tightly to the saddle horn and cast a panicky glance at L. D.'s extended fingers. "Help me, L. D.! Help me!"

Milton's cry was not fully voiced before the bay's forefoot came down hard at rim's edge, but L. D. read the sudden implosion and anticipated the ensuing collapse of a section of shelf in time to shout and lunge for Milton's upthrust arm. They locked hands against wrists, their nails biting into one another, and with a primal yell and a wrenching of his shoulder L. D. held fast to let the headfirst plummet of the horse pull Milton from the saddle.

The pliant limb groaned and bent dramatically as the drag of Milton's leg across the animal's hindquarters set them swinging pendulum-like across the gaping break. L. D. could see Milton's upturned face a contorted mask of pain, and his boots kicking against the yawning canyon like a just-hanged man's.

"I'm slipping!" screamed Milton, slapping his free hand up alongside L. D.'s forearm. "I'm gonna fall! I'm gonna fall!"

L. D. saw it coming, too, sweaty hands sliding against sweaty wrists, but he also felt the supporting crook of his leg begin to roll out along the swaying limb. And suddenly he was out-of-control, helpless in face of the inevitable.

"We're goin', Milton!" he cried.

He heard a great popping and cracking of wood and felt the cedar rip apart at the fork above his thigh. It came just as the arc of their swing carried them out toward the ledge, then the breaking bough made a quick down-and-in thrust toward its splitting stem. To both their cries, L. D. slammed upside-down against the rock face, the sudden shock in his arm telling him of Milton's own savage impact. It wrenched them apart, then L. D. was scraping cliff as he and limb alike tumbled crazily after the younger man.

He saw the lip of the broken rimrock catch Milton after only a few feet, then with horse wreck know-how L. D. fended off the shelf with an arm to roll hard across the deputy's leg and feel the knee dig into his mid-section.

Half-stunned, he lay there at chasm's edge for long moments, thrashing around in the splintered twigs and gasping for air. He heard Milton groaning, and he turned in the direction of the collapsed rimrock to find the rising deputy's all-fours perfectly framing the far, narrowing ledge that threaded onward alongside the rock fortification.

And lying there, a thin dark strip against chalky limestone, was the leather cord he knew Charlie had dropped so calculatingly to lure yet another damned tenderfoot into danger.

They trailed back up-rim, to a building silence but for the rushing wind and strike of hoof and boot against rock. L. D. kept the roan in a walk, allowing Milton to keep pace on foot behind. Not only was L. D.'s knee killing him, but now it seemed that every time the gelding took a step he found one more place that hurt. Hell, he was too damned old and out-of-shape to go falling off cliffs.

He thought about what had just happened, and tried to figure out why in thunder he had risked his neck that way. The episode in the mesquites notwithstanding, he knew he wasn't the stuff heroes were made of, and he dat-blamed sure could have still slept at night without having climbed down that cliff for Milton.

But the answer was already there in those half-forgotten dreams. He'd done it because a cowboy would have, because *Charlie* would have.

Milton's deliberate, trembling words stirred him from his thoughts. "I . . . I was a goner, L. D."

L. D. only stared mutely up the rim over the gelding's nodding head.

"That ledge just broke, all of a sudden. One minute it was there, and the next I could see all the way to the bottom."

Still, L. D. only squinted against the falling sun.

"I was going right off that thing with that horse. I . . . I would have, if you hadn't—"

"Oh hell, Milton," L. D. interrupted sarcastically without even a glance, "just another day at the office for one of you 'certified public peace officers,' wasn't it."

And as Milton fell again into silence behind him, L. D. listened to the drum of the hooves and sank a little inside to a deep breath. *Damn it, why wouldn't I even let him thank me?*

Well up-rim they reached a rocky promontory overlooking the canyon and its far banded wall. Here where L. D. momentarily held the horse, the shelf swerved sharply to the left, rimming a side canyon that cut back deeply into the mesa. L. D. followed the rimrock with his eyes, all the way to the gulch's head and then back out to another promontory across from him. Toward it rode three single-file horsemen who, even at a distance, he identified individually as Syers in the lead, the injured deputy in the middle, and Fowler on drag.

"That's them across there, L. D.," said a subdued Milton.

L. D. watched them move against the dark curtain of cedars to burst one-at-a-time against open sky at the point's extreme, then veer sharply out-of-sight. Just as Fowler began rounding the jutting lip, L. D. suddenly saw the horse's gangly legs prance skittishly as it wheeled one way, then another.

"What's he doing with that horse?" Milton babbled excitedly.

But L. D. already had guessed that something across the main canyon had seized Fowler's attention and induced him to try to rein the animal about. To Milton's continued raving, L. D. whirled to search the far rimrock just in time to glimpse the hindquarters of a horse disappearing into timber. Then a 30.06 boomed, and as the echo played against the distant bluff, L. D. spun again to the promontory to find Fowler's horse burying its head and kicking hind legs wildly to spill rider and rifle hard at cliff's edge.

"Damn! Don't they ever learn anything?" L. D. exclaimed, watching Fowler thrash around under the pawing hooves. Then he turned to measure the impossible rifle shot across-canyon to the timbered rim and shook his head. *Damn, Charlie, is there any trick you* didn't *learn?*

Chapter Thirteen

When L. D. and Milton finally worked their way on around to the far promontory and veered left with the rim, sunlight suddenly glinted from the bordering timber and a rifle barrel thrust out.

"Almost got your damned heads blowed off," growled Syers. "Stay out on that rim and that crazy cowboy's still liable to do it."

L. D. took the horse on through the shielding line of brush to find the ranger, down on one knee, lifting binoculars to study the far rim through a break in the undergrowth. On the carpet of cedar needles beside him, the injured deputy tossed fitfully, clutching his wrist and moaning as sweat streamed down his face. Though L. D.'s own knee punished him with every movement, the officer's wrenched and flushed features demanded immediate attention.

"Deputy, how you makin' it?" he asked.

The man only groaned feverishly, and L. D. looked up at Fowler, who stood cupping his hands in lighting a cigarette. "How long's he been like this?" asked L. D. "He gettin' plenty of water?"

"Just poured some down him," said Fowler, taking a deep drag. He bore an ugly bruise on his cheekbone and caked blood on his fingers. "He keeps getting worse. We're about to move him out in the flat so the helicopter can pick him up."

Milton, lagging, brushed through the timber to reach the small clearing. Fowler looked up with surprise. "What are you doing on foot, deputy? Hearing that single horse come up along the rim, we thought it might be Lyles."

"You men looked skinned up as hell," snapped Syers, who had turned.

Milton stopped beside L. D. and stood with lowered eyes. His fingers quaked as he rubbed one hand over the other. "My horse," he whispered with a tremble. "The cliff, it went over."

Syers cursed. "Sorry damn bunch *I've* got to work with," he snapped, turning to spit against nearby foliage.

L. D. studied Fowler's eyes; he had been formulating what to say ever since he had watched Fowler shoot so impetuously. "Looks like Ernest here did his best to get throwed down in that canyon also," he said with thinly veiled anger.

Fowler flushed. "I don't want to hear it, Sheriff. I'm not going to take anything off of you."

L. D. half-smiled. "Gettin' kind of ill-humored aren't you, Ernest? It couldn't be you're startin' to wonder a little bit about Charlie Lyles hangin' himself on all that rope you've been playin' out, could it? How 'bout you, Syers? Think this is still some drugstore cowboy that'll come ridin' back in at the first saddle sore so you can go make time with that waitress?"

With a sharp breath, L. D. turned away, shaking his head in disgust as the anger built. Then he whirled upon Fowler. "That was a helluva stunt you pulled over there, Ernest, a *helluva* stunt."

Fowler straightened, defensive anger narrowing his eyes. "I told you to lay off of me, Sheriff," he snapped. "You weren't over there—you don't know a damn thing about what was going through my mind." He slung a hand in the direction of the far rim. "I looked over there and he was just sitting there on that horse staring at me. He made some kind of motion with his arm; I thought he was going to shoot, so I had to do something. I had him, and then I couldn't get that damned horse around quick enough to get him in my sights. One more second and I'd've got him."

"But he didn't *give* you that second—so who got who? If that horse of yours had been any closer to the rim, we could've figured that out pretty easy. As it is, the way your face looks and all the places he tore up your shirt pawin' at you tells me plenty. It tells me we're playin' right into Charlie Lyles' hands out here. He knows he don't *hafta* lift a gun, not when he sees a bunch of greenhorns stumblin' around, spookin' their own horses firin' over their ears, runnin' 'em wild as the devil through mesquites, gettin' suckered out on a ledge they can't get off of—Milton can tell you about that, can't you, Milton?"

He passed an all-encompassing hand across the group. "I told you from the start you didn't know who you was dealin' with, and not a damn one of you would listen. *Now* look— yesterday we got one man killed and another one busted up, and ever'body today's either hurt or plain rode into the ground. Meanwhile, Charlie keeps on ridin', and I'll damn sure bet he's no worse for the wear."

"Yeah, you're a big lawman now, Hankins," Syers snapped caustically. "You sit up there on that horse and point out all the things that've gone wrong, like we don't have eyes for ourselves. But I damned sure don't hear any answers coming from you."

L. D. found a deep breath; he was so damned tired he didn't know how many deep breaths he had left. "Charlie Lyles is out there trying to break us, and from the looks of ever'body he's doin' a pretty good job at it. What we need more than anything is rest. Like I said before, I can get it out here, but y'all don't know how. Y'all need to go back in, get a good night's sleep."

"Like hell," snarled Syers. He stood, weak-kneed, and studied Fowler and Milton. "You men add everything up— it's not like we're out here on some deer hunt; there's a man out there killed a fellow law enforcement officer, and it damned sure could've been any one of us just as well. If we go off relaxing and he gets away, it shows every punk in the state with a gun that he can shoot a cop and not pay the consequences. I'm damned sure not willing to let that happen like Hankins is."

"Quit playin' jury, Syers," snapped L. D. "It's awful convenient the way you keep forgettin' we don't know that Charlie Lyles killed anybody."

"Hell," interjected Fowler, "he almost got *me* killed."

L. D. felt the blood rush to his face. "That was your own fault, goin' and shootin' like a damned fool."

Fowler ignored the comment. "Syers has a point. There won't even *be* a jury if we don't bring him in—and we can't do that lying around some motel. After they pick my deputy up, let's get the chopper crew to bring us out some blankets, more food and water. I'm as sore and burned up as anybody else, but I'm willing to tough it out one more day. I brought him in before and I intend to be there when we do it again."

L. D. breathed sharply and looked down, shaking his head. Then he lifted his eyes and found Milton. "How 'bout you, Milton?" he asked impatiently, remembering more the displaced loyalty than the clasp of their hands above that canyon.

"You're my boss, L. D."

L. D. looked away, sinking a little in reflection on the brush with death they had shared. *Damn it, Milton, is that the best you can say?*

Charlie's flight from the whizzing bullet carried him up-rim into heavy timber. At the first hint of a canyon-side break, he held the horse and looked across the gorge through shimmering greenery to see Fowler rolling around underneath his spooked and pawing animal. Then Charlie was off again, bearing away from the canyon in anticipation of an imminent sweep by the helicopter.

He loped the horse into a sudden, oak-walled clearing with stumps and prickly pear, and moments before he ducked back into the brush, his horse kicked through an old fire ring of gray-smoked rock. To the side, he glimpsed scattered flint chips, sparkling in the sunlight like tiny silver conchos. Then he was inside the timber, holding his horse and peering up through the limbs at the bubble of the helicopter sweeping overhead.

But at the same time, he was reflecting on those long-forgotten Indians who had found in these canyons and mesas a home—just as he was trying to do. Their lives had been brutal and short, by the white man's standards, and not even tombstones had marked their passing. But maybe that end had been fitting for such a people: returning quietly to dust, replenishing the Earth in thanks for first giving them life, and then cradling them all their days.

Maybe, too, he mused, it would be a fitting end for a cowboy. After all, in this backcountry he had felt a measure of real peace for the first time ever, as though a powerful and benevolent spirit pastured here. In every green-belted canyon and banded bluff, every highland flat and forested drainage, even in the rustle of leaves and breath of sun-baked cedar, he had come to know the Earth in the way spoken of by that Comanche he had branded with one spring just over the county line near Greenleaf.

Through mesquites and oaks they had ridden side-by-side, bound for the back corner and a roundup drive. "See the land?" the Indian with the broad, aging face had asked. His hat shaded dark, sad eyes, and angular lines underscored his heavy cheekbones. "You look at it every day, but did you ever really see it? The old men used to call it Pia—*Mother."*

"How come?" asked Charlie.

"When I was a boy, the Nermernuh—*our People—would talk about how it gives us everything we eat and makes the streams run. One* tsukup', *old man, liked to ask me, '*Tua'—*that's like 'son'—'Tua, what's to keep the ground hard, to*

hold these horses up? Or lets the grass just sprout up without anybody planting it? Pia, Mother-Earth.' He'd say, *'Think about it—all these horses couldn't eat, or the wild game or me or you, if it wasn't that way.'*

"But even the Nermernuh *had to go way out alone to ever see it. The* tsukup' *used to go looking for a spirit to give them* puha, *medicine. They used to have visions. Maybe only the old* Nermernuh *can have visions. But go way out far, by yourself, and it's like the Earth's alive. It's* Pia, *our Mother, and she gives us life and lets us drink her milk, and all she wants in return is that, when we die, we go on back to her— just like our soul goes back to the Spirit who made Mother-Earth."*

Charlie had never been religious. Certainly, his upbringing had not been conducive to a spiritual life, and seven-day weeks in a succession of isolated cow camps had ruled out any notions of church attendance. In fact, Charlie had never even known a religious cowboy. Moral men, yes, and honest and trustworthy, but never a religious one in the evangelical sense. But, on the other hand, he had never known a cowboy who outright denied God's existence either. Before a couple of days ago, Charlie had never thought about it much; he had supposed he believed in God, and, as a natural extension, in the Son of God. But now, amid a desperate chase and inner turmoil, he had begun to feel as if he no longer rode alone, as if before him, leading and filling him with *puha*, went a Spirit he was coming to know in a personal way.

But where there was a God, giving life and bringing peace, there was also a devil, trying to snatch it all away just as it was almost within his grasp. And he couldn't help wondering just where L. D. fit in in all of this.

Hell, L. D., don't you even know me anymore? he asked silently across the distance. *I rode out of your world and washed my hands of it. Now I'm here where I can wake up of a mornin' and know I fit in, know I'm right where I ought to have been a hundred years ago. And damn it, L. D., I'll be a*

SOB if I go spurrin' this horse somewhere else till the land itself starts tellin' me to.

With the frame of mind of the hunter, rather than the hunted, Charlie waited patiently in the timber, and finally the helicopter veered back across-canyon with the same abruptness as it had come. To a serenade of cicadas he rode northward on into the coming of twilight, cutting through two fences as he flanked canyons and dipped into gullies that marked their heads. He stayed in the brush where possible, and traversed the inevitable open grasslands in quick bursts that lathered and winded his horse. He could feel the strength wrenched from the animal with every stride, and for the first time he felt a twinge of regret that so many horses paid the price for a cowboy's dreams.

But, damn it, that's not the way he'd wanted it.

In one grassy stretch he passed a buzzard perching in a dead mesquite. Charlie watched the vulture flap a wing and lift its sharp, powerful talons to claw at its own feathers, and he remembered another "guaranteed sign" the old cowboys had sworn by: *when a buzzard on a stump scratches itself, look for a flash flood in less than a day.*

Dusk found Charlie on rimrock facing north. Shadows blanketed the canyon below, and crept out across the breaks to the northeast like a great, black fog. Out of it rose the folded bluffs of the caprock, rolling away red-tinted in the sunset's afterglow, while a dominating, bony ridge stood far away against the northern horizon. The latter topographic feature Charlie recognized as Green Mountain, though he had never seen it except from the perspective of the railroad tracks and open country on the other side. He couldn't help thinking how ironic that he should find it looming ahead, this hogback joined to the Divide only by a ribbon of land. The Indian had once pointed it out and told him something about a medicine man being buried there, something about long-ago Comanches journeying to its southern slope in vision quests for power and understanding.

Charlie didn't know about that, but he did yearn for a time and place in which understanding came as simply as fasting a few days on a mountain.

He turned the horse down through a break in the rimrock and plunged it toward the cedars with jags of dead limbs.

An instant before he heard the rattler, he smelled it, a quick whiff laced with the pungency of a just-forged horseshoe in a blacksmith's shop. Then the maraca-like vibration reared his horse to a frightened snorting, catching the reins loose in Charlie's hand, and suddenly animal and rider alike were crashing off-balance down the brushy bands of rimrock. Cedars cracked and popped before them, a gray pitchfork of dead limbs exploding in Charlie's face. Then he could only bury his head along the gelding's neck and cling to the saddle horn for the wildest ride of his life, knowing from the brand-like fire down along his throat that he was hurt badly.

They made it to the canyon floor, a spooked horse and a shaken cowboy, and when Charlie ran his hand up alongside his adam's apple, his fingers grew warm and sticky with blood. He turned his head slightly, and red droplets splattered his thigh and the upper part of the stirrup. They seemed to come in spurts that coincided with the hammering of his heart, and all he could do was clamp his hand against his neck and dismount, suddenly feeling a little afraid and very alone.

He propped the rifle against a bush and forced himself to unbridle and stake the bay with one hand, then sank to the shadows. He could feel the blood oozing hot and moist from beneath his palm. He found his pocketknife and opened it with his teeth, then awkwardly slashed and ripped the tail from his shirt. Removing his hat, which somehow had survived the ride, he placed it on his thighs and set about scraping it, watching the felt collect like sawdust on the brim. The old-timers had told him about how the shavings might stifle a bloody flow. Charlie wasn't sure about that, but as he sprinkled the shavings onto the rag and pressed it tightly against his throbbing neck, he at least took comfort in knowing it was a cowboy's way.

He suddenly shivered to a strange chill like the prick of a thousand spur rowels filed needle-sharp, and as he grew lightheaded he leaned back against a rock outcropping and watched the horse swim before him. For more than forty-eight hours now, ever since he had ridden into this wilderness, he had been so sure of himself, so confident that at last he had found a cowboy's world and never would be driven from it. But as the blood continued to soak a stream down his shirt and the world seemed to drift away, a little at a time, self-doubts gnawed at him and he began to question all his actions, wonder if he would make it.

He *had* to, for he knew there was no other way for a cowboy to live.

Just as there was no other way for one to die.

Chapter Fourteen

Sharing the dusk with his bedroll, L. D. sat with one knee upraised and stared down along his stiff, outstretched leg at his once-lustrous boot, now as scuffed as an old cattle trail. Damn, he was tired and beaten, tortured by the push across one last canyon to these flats where Charlie had drawn fire. The details of the camp crept into his peripheral vision only as if through a thick fog. There was Milton, off to his right, prone on an army surplus sleeping bag; Fowler, in the opposite direction, drenching his upturned face with water from a plastic jug; and Syers, a dozen feet beyond L. D.'s uplifted boot toe, sitting drooped in an exhausted stupor over the semi-automatic rifle in his lap.

Likewise blurred by the ordeal of two days were the saddles, positioned as pillows before each man's bedding, and the geldings—one still saddled for a night horse—staked to nearby mesquites. Just the cicadas, with their incessant buzzing, impacted L. D.'s senses much, and they only because the drone reminded him of all the evenings he had sat on his front porch in audience to their serenade and dwelled on the idealism of youth he had let slip away.

You're the one got me out here, Charlie, he said silently. *You got me out here finally livin' all those damned dreams I had once upon a time, Goodnight and the Pecos and that whole bit.* He rubbed his badly swollen knee, shifted to ease the pressure on the building saddle sores, groaned to the aches of a bad horse wreck and jarring fall down a cliff. *Damn it, that's just where I should've left it all too—in my dreams. Hell, Charlie, why couldn't you have just left 'em there too?*

He turned his head slightly at a coyote's yip-yip-yip that became a long, mournful howl.

"Damned wolves," muttered Syers tiredly, without raising his head. "Wish they'd shut up that damned yapping."

"Been howling that way ever since we topped out of that canyon," droned Fowler, rustling a topographic map as he unrolled it into the beam of his flashlight.

"Sun wasn't even down then," said L. D. "Charlie always said if they go to howling in the daytime, we got some bad weather comin'."

Syers looked up and exhaled in disgust. "It's always 'Charlie this' and 'Charlie that,'" he snapped. "Didn't you ever learn to think for yourself?"

L. D. stared through the dusk at him. "I learned plenty quick out on the JAs it paid to listen to him. Like those wore-down horses actin' so frolicky when we unsaddled 'em— he'd point somethin' like that out and tell me to keep my slicker handy, and sure enough, here'd come a big rain in a day or so."

"Hell, nothing but partly cloudy skies in the forecast," said Syers.

A map again rustled in Fowler's hands; L. D. looked over to find him unscrolling it on the ground beside three other topos whose corners curled against restraining rocks. "We've just crossed over into another quadrangle," said the Jim Ned County sheriff. He traced a finger up the line of maps, the flashlight beam following. "Still headed pretty much north. Country doesn't look any easier ahead either, not till up past Green Mountain where it's clear sailing to that railroad and blacktop."

Milton lifted his head from the saddle. "Ever hear them talk about Green Mountain, that long skinny ridge?" Weariness slurred his words. "You have, L. D., how the Indians thought it was sacred or something. I'd just as soon give all those Indian spooks a wide berth."

Through the building dark L. D. turned his eyes to the north. *Green Mountain—is that what this is all about, Charlie? Is that where you been headin' all along, and maybe didn't even know it yourself? Hell, Charlie, you're ridin' for the high lonesome, aren't you, out on a vision quest like that big talk of the old Comanche you told me about workin' with up at Greenleaf.*

Hard dark choked all but a few shadowy outlines. Only that of Syers, on first watch with Ruger clutched tightly, remained distinguishable to L. D. Even after L. D. joined the other two men in sinking to a lumpy bedroll, and turned his tired eyes to find tiny tails of light clinging to every star, the image of the semi-automatic rifle would not go away. *Good God, Charlie*, he thought, closing his eyes and feeling himself drawn toward a deep, deep sleep, *don't . . . get . . . in . . . front . . . of . . . those . . . sights. . . .*

A sound familiar to him through a thousand days on the JAs followed him into the stage between wakefulness and full sleep, then Syers' quick "What the hell was that?" startled him. He burst to an elbow, his temples suddenly pounding as he whirled with the other men's silhouettes at the ranger's cry.

The familiar sound came again; L. D. saw the steel of Syers' rifle swing toward it. "Over there!" cried the ranger.

L. D. exhaled in disgust. "Good gosh a-mighty, y'all hold your damned fire for once, will you?"

"I heard it, too, L. D.!" Milton exclaimed excitedly. "There's something over there!"

L. D. breathed sharply. "Yeah, there's somethin' over there all right, Milton—our own night horse shakin' his saddle. But guess y'all are gettin' pretty good at shootin' horses by now, aren't you? Whatsamatter, Syers, you afraid of somethin' all the time?"

"Hell, no, I'm not afraid of something—I'm afraid of *everything*. It's when you go to trusting what's out there in the dark, or on the street, the guy behind you on the sidewalk, that you end up with a knife in your gut or your brains blown out."

"It's nice to know," said L. D., "that you've got such a positive view of ever'body."

"Let me tell you three little rules about law enforcement, Hankins," said Syers condescendingly. "Expect the worst from everybody. Look everybody in the eye and make sure they know you're not backing down no matter what. And don't be afraid to knock the hell out of somebody or pull the trigger when the situation calls for it. If you're not up to all that, maybe you better trade that badge in for a social worker's card.

"Now, that SOB out there's trying to rub our noses in the dirt—and I don't take that off *anybody.* Yeah, one time I might've thought like you—give everybody the benefit of the doubt; just show them you trust them and they won't let you down. Like *hell* they won't. I was working a bar one night, a rookie deputy up in Fort Worth. Four or five Meskins were standing over another one in the parking lot, kicking the hell out of him, and here I came with all these big ideas about how everybody's just a good old boy if you just give him a break. I thought I could handle it all just by letting them see my badge, relying on their respect for authority, so I didn't call for a backup or even gesture with that big billy club of a flashlight, much less pull my revolver. Well, the SOBs turned on me and beat the hell out of me, busted two ribs, bruised a kidney, knocked out some teeth. I damn near died when one of those ribs went through my lung. When I got out of the hospital, I swore that wouldn't ever happen again, that from here on out every bastard I went after was guilty till somebody proved them innocent. So I don't give anybody a break anymore, because they're damned sure not going to give *me* one—and that includes you and any crazy cowboy riding around out there."

L. D. had sat up to stare through the dark at the ranger. "At least there's one way you're like the old-time cowboys,

Syers. Back then, if they liked you they showed it, and if they didn't like you, they told you up front."

Fowler cursed quietly. "You're really hung up on cowboys, aren't you, Sheriff," he criticized. "It's been my experience that all these cowboys working these ranches aren't equal to a ten-year-old boy when they get to town and go to drinking."

L. D. found his shadowy outline. "I'm talkin' about *real* cowboys, Ernest, the kind that don't exist no more—except for one."

"Yeah?" said Fowler caustically. "Maybe you don't know about Charlie Lyles coming into Angelo and getting drunker than a fiddler's bitch, tearing up a bar or two. They say he stayed drunk half the time working those ranches."

"You've seen all that?" cross-examined L. D. with implied doubt.

"I've heard about it."

"Just like you've heard about him shootin' Powers, I suppose. You believe the parts you want to believe because you're too damned lazy to check it out for yourself."

Fowler's shadow straightened. "You're getting damn far out of line, Sheriff."

"Well, I'll tell you, Ernest, it seems to me a lawman ought to be a little more responsible in what he takes for truth. Now, I worked with Charlie for quite a spell, and a person got fired on the JAs for three things, and that was for drinking and fighting and gambling—and Charlie never did get fired. Now, he'd drink a little, all right, when we went to town, but he held his liquor good and knew when to set the bottle down. Most people don't—and that includes you, Ernest. I remember a time when you were three sheets to the wind out dove hunting."

He only heard Fowler breathe sharply.

Mutual exhaustion curbed any further exchange, and with a deep sigh L. D. fell back on his bedroll. But now, troubled thoughts knotted his stomach. A grim blackness that had nothing to do with the night spread over him like a shroud. He wished he'd never had any part of this. He wished he could just walk away from it all like Sarah had said and let what was going to happen, happen. It was going to anyway. They were going to kill Charlie. Tomorrow, they were going to kill him. There was no other way for this to end.

Saturday, June 5
When the shifting of his horse's hooves against rock woke Charlie, his neck felt drawn and flies were blowing him.

He seemed to have to summon a lot of energy just to brush one from his lip, and even more to roll over groggily on the blood-stained rocks to see, by daylight, the horse shying and tugging at the pliant greenery holding the rope. What in Sam Hill—

He dragged himself to his hip, then stiffened at the sudden ragged turbulence of helicopter rotors. He whirled skyward, catching the glint of sunlight against the craft as it burst out over the rim. Then with a great rush of adrenalin he was on his feet and reeling-in the bay at the length of the stake rope. Gaining the animal, he quickly fitted the headstall and bit in place and slipped the loop of the rope free, leaving it where it dropped. He seized the rifle and, within seconds, was astride the horse, spurring it lightly in the belly, turning it down the forested canyon bottom.

Damn it, they seen you! he cursed himself as his horse went crashing through the underbrush. *You stayed out in the open and now they come along and seen you!*

It wasn't excuse enough that he had been badly hurt, and maybe still was, or that he had lapsed into unconsciousness right where he had slid off the gelding. He was a cowboy who should have damned well coped better.

He broke through a wall of briars at the canyon drainage and turned the horse down through a curving rock chute. Drifts of browned leaves padded the gelding's gait for a few strides, then the drainage widened and the hooves sent scattered rocks skimming along. The way grew so tangled with overhanging greenery and deadfall that he could only guard his throat and let the gelding plow through, yet even with a great cracking of limbs in his ears he could hear only the choppy whir above.

Well downstream, a drift dam in the drainage turned his horse up through a small clearing on the slope. He took a moment to look back and up, past the tops of elms thrashing in a wave before the sweeping rotors, and saw them on the rim. There were four of them, all astride those comparatively fresh horses. Only one of the men carried himself in the saddle anything like a cowboy, and he—L. D.—rode like he had a boil on his backside. But damn it, tenderfeet or not, they had those fresher horses and were right on his tail.

Charlie gigged the bay back into the shaded drainage and on down-canyon, where another window opened up through the wind-swept foliage and allowed him a second look back.

He'd hoped he'd shaken them. He'd hoped like hell he had. He'd hoped he'd broken their will, sent them beaten and broken back into their own world. But there they were, coming off the rim, three men on foot leading their horses, and L. D. still astride his.

Fresher horses.

The thought stuck in his mind as he turned away and again touched the bay with his spurs.

Fresher horses.

And he on a rode-down gelding that, in the moments of desperation the night before, he had not even relieved of its saddle. Even worse, he didn't feel right; he seemed a little feverish, and up from his throat burned a great thirst that even a long swig from the jug couldn't quench. A fire seemed to radiate from the tightness at his blood-caked neck and consume his shoulder and upper chest. Every time he bore any weight in the stirrups he felt as wobbly-legged as a just-foaled colt. He felt drained of all energy, powerless to do anything but hang on and let the bay carry him on out into the breaks.

For the first time since he had come seeking the lost Old West in these hidden canyons, the voices of self-doubt echoed through his mind.

Give it up, Charlie, we've got you beat.

He pushed the bay harder through the underbrush and heard the animal breathe in frenzied gasps that racked its frame.

The Old West doesn't exist anymore, Charlie, not for you, not for anybody.

He heard the growing din of helicopter rotors and dodged a sudden downdraft that set his horse shying.

There's no place to run, Charlie, there's no place to run.

He wheeled the horse up out of the drainage into the timber masking the widening canyon. A sudden lightheadedness set the horse's mane swimming before him and sent the sun spinning crazily through the limbs. He clutched the saddle horn and fell across it, yet a part of him still seemed to drift away, separating awareness of self from body until only the fire in his throat tethered the two.

You're gonna die out here, Charlie, you're gonna die.

It looked as if the voices were right—but he was just glad that, if he could never live like a cowboy, at least he might die like one.

Chapter Fifteen

L. D. ran his fingers across the blood-stained rock that testified to Charlie's desperate night repose and withdrew them pale and trembling. *You're in trouble, Charlie*, he thought, studying the trail of broken limbs down from the bluff above. *Damn it, Charlie, you're in bad trouble.*

"Must've had him in your sights better than you thought, Sheriff Fowler," Milton said from behind.

Syers spat a stream to the blood darkening the canyon floor. "We've got him; this time we've *got* the SOB. You hear me, Hankins? He's out there bleeding like a strung-up goat with its throat slit, and between us and the chopper and the units headed for those canyon roads, he's got no place to go but hell."

L. D. didn't say anything. What *was* there to say, when he was kneeling there staring at Charlie's blood?

"Let's mount up and get after him," said Fowler. "This whole damn thing can't end any too soon for me. I never had to shoot anybody before and I'm not proud I had to do it now."

L. D. rose, grimacing to the pain in his knee, and reached for the stirrup of his horse. "In case you're keepin' score or somethin', Ernest," he said caustically, without even honoring him with a glance, "you've now shot just as many men out here as Charlie has—and that's none. Now, swaybacked *horses* are somethin' else."

"That man's been bleeding like hell—can't you see that?" snapped Fowler.

L. D. could see it, all right—which was why he only mounted up and turned the gelding down-canyon instead of arguing the point. Charlie *had* bled like hell, and it damned sure didn't matter why.

Again, the chase was on, this time through a tangled wilderness of briary elms and cedars, drift dams, and deadfall. The upward-crawling sun that found its way through was warm and life-giving, yet to L. D. there seemed a deep gloom choking the canyon. *Blood*, he thought as he plunged the horse down the drainage through crackling brush, *Charlie's blood*. He saw it again on that rock, and the dark stains seemed to go with him, repeatedly exploding into his mind like one calf after another bolting out of a roping chute. He had taken the gelding to the forefront simply by his better horsemanship, but he rode drained of all energy and even of caring. He wished it were over. He wished they were already riding back in to the trailers with Charlie's body draped across a horse. That's how it was all going to end anyway. One second, Charlie would be a living, breathing, hoping individual with yearnings not much different from his own, and the next second he would be dead.

And with him would die—for both of them—the last of those damned dreams.

He whirled with fire in his eyes to the trailing riders. He couldn't take any more. The worry, the anticipation, the dread, the war going on inside him and the one taking place before his eyes—damn it, he couldn't take any more! Just let the SOBs shoot him and get it all over with!

The long lonesome howl of a coyote from the breaks turned him again to the drainage, just in time to feel his horse shy at a rattlesnake slithering up the bank. *Coyotes in daytime and rattlers goin' for high ground—bad weather a-comin', just like you used to tell me, Charlie, back when there was still a halfway place for you.*

A limb twisted with thorny vines raked his cheek, and with the sudden sting came a curse of self-condemnation. *Hell, wouldn't there still be a place for Charlie if I'd just told Milton to go to hell the night he came over?*

Then, within the next quarter-mile, L. D. came upon three dry-land terrapins and a couple of toads—more "guaranteed signs," Charlie had said—and at the next break in the leafy canopy he reined his horse about to find only bright skies above the high-walled bluffs.

Hell, Charlie, do you know what you're talkin' about? Did you ever? Not just about storms comin', but about everything, *horses and the eighteen hundreds and the whole damned cowboyin' bit? What the hell's the matter with you for thinkin' like that, Charlie? What the hell's the matter with me for ever listenin' to you?*

He fell back to the saddle-weary others to catch the crackling sign-off of the chopper pilot over the radio and Syers' vehement curse.

"What is it?" asked L. D., blocking the drainage and forcing them to pull rein.

"Chopper lost him again, L. D.," spoke up Milton. "He must've holed up under one of these trees—look up there, you can't even hardly see daylight sometimes."

"Maybe he bled to death, got so weak he couldn't ride," suggested Fowler.

Syers cursed again. "SOB's still out there, all right," he said, lifting his eyes down-canyon. "If that chopper can't see that horse moving around, you can bet it's because the SOB's holding him in under this brush."

"Ought to be able to hear it nicker every once in a while if that's the case," said Milton.

"Over *that* racket?" asked Fowler, nodding in the direction of the chopper's whir. "Topo map doesn't show this thing to have any side canyons—why not have the helicopter back off a little, guard down-canyon? If that horse will nicker or shake his saddle and clue us in, I'm all for it. The way this canyon's starting to widen, all we can do is spread out and try to flush him out. That's a desperate, wounded man with a rifle out there, and they don't pay me enough to go get my head blowed off."

"Y'all can do whatever it is you want to," said L. D., his voice drained of emotion, "but I want you to get me a weather forecast 'fore you do it."

"Hell, Hankins, you're not even subtle about it anymore," snarled Syers. "Get that horse out of my damned way. I'm backing that chopper off and we're spreading out and getting that SOB—with or without you." And he brushed his horse past L. D.'s and on up the right-side bank.

L. D. noticed Fowler's gelding suddenly spook a little, and he saw a toad go hopping between the forelegs. And again came memories and doubts about Charlie and about himself, and he sank a little more inside and turned his horse after Syers.

"Oh, L. D.," called out Milton, "we did pick up an updated afternoon forecast while ago from the dispatcher."

L. D. held up his horse and, lethargically, looked around to find Milton's eyes.

"Thunderstorms," said the deputy. "*Severe* thunderstorms."

L. D. gigged his horse hard for the bordering brush.

Mid afternoon. A weak horse and weaker rider struggling up a timbered slope to hesitate before exposed rimrock swept by dust. Bloodshot eyes looking back at the canyon through a tangle of swaying limbs. The grainy air an oven, setting the distant bands of rock dancing in heat waves. And the sun a fireball in stark contrast to the massive thunderhead, dark-swirled beside it, that jutted up over the cedared ridge to the southwest.

It all came to Charlie through an inner haze, and at times he still rode strangely distant to his own body, but he doggedly held on to awareness and reason. The two told him that he had to get out of this canyon, keep riding deeper into the backcountry, somehow elude the pursuing riders and the dust devil that for anxious minutes that morning had thrashed the woodland about him. In desperation he had reined his horse in under a windbreak to rub the lathered neck and gently soothe with quiet, calm tones. Then, unaccountably, the chopper had withdrawn, and once more he had spurred the gelding down the broadening canyon that trended north-eastward. On through early afternoon he had clung to the horse like a bulldogging ranch hand to the horns of a mean-tempered steer. The bay had broken trail for miles through the brush until the bordering bluffs had begun to fall away dramatically. Then the faint whir of the helicopter from the canyon mouth and the nicker of a horse from up-canyon had turned Charlie and the gelding up the slope.

The trailing horses were quiet now, but the chopper's steady drone, from an indeterminate distance away, held him in this last shielding brush for long seconds before he pushed on up into the sunlight and through a breach in the rock. He broke over the blustery rim to feel the sting of sand from behind and face a scorched veldt, dotted dark green with scrub cedar, unfurling toward Green Mountain's hazy spine. It rose and fell abruptly a few miles away, yet the ominous peak of the thunderhead at Charlie's shoulder dwarfed it. And even while suddenly feeling strangely drawn toward that hogback in a desperate longing for understanding, he wondered if the land itself hadn't begun whispering for him to leave.

He knew that something, too, had whispered in the gelding's ear; the animal had cold-jawed when he had first tried to turn it up the slope, and even now, it wanted to bear eastward, away from the rising cloud. Charlie knew a horse's instinct to flee a storm, and judging by the way the tired animal fought the reins, he realized this one had to be a booger. Furthermore, the rumble of thunder reminded him that, out here in the open, he'd have to take his chances with lightning, which would strike a man on horseback before it would anything else.

He took the gelding on out from the rim, and knew he was in trouble the instant the animal shied. Then the sudden swelling of whirring rotors in his dulled ears turned him down-canyon just in time to see the helicopter's silvery bubble burst over the rim a quarter-mile away.

"Hyahhhh!"

He spurred the bay and the two fled across the grassland to the drum of the animal's hooves. The shadows of horse and rider leaped to the forefront and cut a path through side oats grama and horse nettle, over prickly pear and sharp-pronged bear grass, past lone dead mesquites and cedar shrubs. Charlie hung on by pure instinct, and through his legs he could feel the pace wrenching the gelding's strength with every hammer of its heart.

Charlie knew a good horse when he saw one. He knew this one to be a cow horse that could cut a tomcat out of a stove pipe. But he also knew a suffering horse. And this gelding, after carrying his weight and that of a saddle for most of three days now in the most rugged country he had ever seen, was fading fast.

But no faster than he. And suddenly he thought about the JA horse they had called *Regular Mi Cuenta*—"Regulate My Account" or "Figure Up My Time"—as one fed-up cowboy had told the boss after the animal had pitched him off on one too many occasions. And Charlie couldn't help but wonder if, in somebody's tally book, his own time wasn't being figured up right this moment.

He didn't have to look back to know the chopper was quickly closing on him; the building thrash of rotors told him plenty. The din reached its utmost at the moment of a violent downdraft that set the gelding throwing its ears out and bowing its back under Charlie's thighs. Charlie read the signs just in time to fight back fiercely on the reins with a backward lean and a hard push against the saddle horn—leverage that alone kept the spooked horse from burying its head and pitching. Then the chopper was past him, rising, arcing back across the sky.

It cut a swath across the dark backdrop of the thunder-head and disappeared behind him. It was a reprieve only long enough for him to sight a mott of chittam trees at ten o'clock and push the gelding hard for it. With the change of angle, their racing shadows veered right, then died in blanketing shade. To the growl of clouds and the bite of grainy gusts scented with rain, he slapped the bay alongside the neck, asking the animal for more than it had to give. Then the bedlam of rotors rose again in his ears, and a second, even-more-furious downdraft set him ducking.

From behind, something struck him a hard, glancing blow on the shoulder, and as it drove him forward, whipping his neck, he caught sight of the chopper's landing skid sailing on and up before him. Then his face was in the gelding's mane, his cheek bouncing and sliding down along the foamy neck. For a frantic moment he hung there, more off than on, then the flailing hooves came flying up and he was just too weak to do anything but let it happen.

In the canyon bottom, L. D. fell back to the radio to hear for himself the frenzied voice crying out over the background roar of the chopper.

Charlie. Up on top. Armed and riding like hell. One sweep, then another. Bumped off hard, maybe hurt. Dragged by the reins yet holding on. Regaining control, crawling for a house-sized chittam mott, pulling the horse in after him. The chopper dipping, dropping off a trooper to the cover of a big stand of prickly pear twenty yards from the grove. The craft rising again, circling, thrashing the trees, guarding the back.

Syers slapped the radio back to its holster and reined his horse up the side of the canyon. "SOB's shot his wad for good this time!" he cried with a glance in L. D.'s direction. "Get the others on up here!"

But L. D. already had turned his gelding after him and wasn't about to go back now. "You tell those men up there not to go pushin' him or somebody'll die! You hear me, Syers! *Somebody'll die!"*

But the ranger just kept on urging his horse up the slope to a cracking of limbs and sloughing of ledges.

The course up through the breaches in the rimrock would not permit two horses abreast, forcing L. D. to settle for being second over the stormy rim. Dead ahead, the ranger's animal already was pulling away in a lope, while beyond the foamy hindquarters, the wind rolled through the grasses for several hundred yards, all the way to a mott of chittams. Between it and the huge stand of prickly pear to its right, a blur of gray uniform suddenly caught L. D.'s eye, and he went cold as he realized it was the trooper, diving toward the grove.

L. D. already knew it was too late even as he spurred his horse. *Good God, Charlie! They're gonna force you to do it!* he cried silently, watching the rifle-wielding trooper strike the ground in a roll and spring up into a guerrilla-like position behind an outer chittam. *The damned fool's goin' and tryin' to be a hero and they're gonna force you to do it!*

L. D. quickly overtook Syers and passed him, but now as he looked with dread anticipation on the unfolding scene, the gelding beneath him suddenly seemed suspended in an ever-widening veldt even though he had the animal in a furious gallop. There wasn't going to be time! The damned fool was pushing Charlie over the edge and there wasn't going to be time to stop it!

The shaded grassland before him brightened for an instant, and a few more strides brought sudden, deafening thunder. He whirled, feeling the smart of the first big raindrops in his face, and saw an ominous cloud rolling in, low and dark-hued. Already, it seemed to hover over the timbered rim up-canyon as if to smother it, while the clouds above—backlighted by the sun and red-tinted by sand—tossed to the deep-throated roll of thunder.

There's your storm, Charlie! he cried silently. *Just like you always told me!*

He set his eyes again on the mott, which still seemed so far away. He had closed to within a hundred yards when a staccato outburst of events ahead brought him unconsciously reining up in stunned, helpless surveillance.

The trooper. Spinning from the tree. Dropping before a cactus at a break in the thicket's shadowy wall. Springing up with a quick brandish of the rifle. The hint of a step forward, then a recoiling. The head and breast of a horse suddenly exploding out of the dark and rearing with its rider. Forelegs flailing air, the hooves catching the shrinking trooper in the shoulder, the ribs, the chest, despite the parrying arms. A blow to the neck felling him, then hooves dropping to trample squirming legs as the horse bolted through the wind and rain.

Charlie!

Another loud peal of thunder set L. D.'s horse wheeling, and then Syers suddenly was at his shoulder, the .223 swinging out over the angular head of L. D.'s spooked animal and discharging between its ears. L. D. and the gelding recoiled at the booming *rat-a-tat-tat* that kicked up little clods of turf at the hooves of the fleeing horse, and even as the first whiff of gun smoke singed L. D.'s nostrils, the world suddenly began rushing by and tossing crazily. He reached for the rain-slick saddle horn and winced at the jarring blows that seemed to wrench every bone in his back and neck. Abruptly he seemed to be astride only air, and as he went off-balance, the cantle reached up to rake the inside of his leg. He looked to see thrashing hooves and grass hurtling up. At the last moment he felt his foot drive forward in the stirrup and lock with a sharp, twisting pain, then the ground slammed hard against his back and shoulder.

And suddenly he was fighting for his life under a boot and spur hung to a runaway horse.

Dragged!

Chapter Sixteen

L. D. knew he had three chances.

Syers could head off the horse. His boot could come off. His spur strap could break.

He wouldn't have bet a plug nickel on any of them, but he knew if anything was going to happen, it had better happen damned quick, or it would be *adiós amigo*.

Already he was bouncing and jumping through the damp grass like a rider tied to the back of a mean-pitching bronc, and it was only a matter of time before he uprooted a stump or caught a hoof or rock in the skull. He thought about Sarah and hoped she wouldn't see him if he didn't make it; back on the JAs one night, a horse had dragged a man until the mesquites and rocks had stripped him bare and bloody and peeled his face to the point that he was no longer recognizable.

Three chances.

No! Charlie wouldn't just lie there, letting the horse drag the hell out of him! He'd climb back up on the saddle, or cut the stirrup leather with his knife, or shoot the clabberhead. He might die anyway, but he damned sure wouldn't go quietly!

L. D. had just begun fighting for his pocketknife when his spur strap broke.

The hooves flew away from him and he went tumbling and rolling out through the wet grass. Lightning cracked and he found himself squirming under a dark sky and wincing at the light rain in his eyes. He pulled his hand up from the fold of fat bulging through his ripped shirt and saw the raindrops make the blood on his fingers run.

He just wanted to lie there. He hurt so damned much he just wanted to roll around groaning and cursing under his breath until he died. The only thing was, he was just too damned mad to do it.

He heard the quick drumming of hooves from behind and turned to catch sudden turf in his face as Syers galloped his horse past. He wrenched himself up to an elbow and turned his eyes after the ranger, and through a building sandstorm he saw Charlie riding slumped over his horse with a one hundred fifty-yard lead.

L. D. whirled to more rising hoofbeats and found Fowler and Milton almost upon him and pushing their horses hard in pursuit. He saw the young deputy's ashen face and wild eyes, saw the thirty-eight rising in his hand, heard his frantic "Shoot him! Shoot him! Shoot him!" Then the two horses were thundering by and shying at the sudden *blam! blam! blam!* of the revolver.

L. D. was on his feet, gritting his teeth to the pain. "Put that damned gun away, Milton!" he yelled.

Dragging the reins, L. D.'s horse had trotted off toward the chittam mott, and with a curse he began limping after it. He knew it was hard enough even with a grain bucket and rope to catch a free-running horse; for a cripple trying to corral one spooked by storm and gunfire, it was just about impossible.

Ahead, he saw Fowler veer for the mott and the writhing trooper, leaving Milton to pull away, still ranting and wildly brandishing the revolver. The damned idiot! He was going to get somebody killed, didn't he know that? And here L. D. was, helpless to do anything but hobble around like a stove-up old cowboy.

He had to do something; good God, he had to *do* something. He looked through a sudden, drenching rain to find Charlie swallowed and Syers only a ghostly shadow. He turned to the mott, where Fowler had dismounted to attend to the trooper wallowing in the mud. And suddenly, L. D. found himself much nearer Fowler's horse—pawing nervously at the ground beside the two—than he did his own. And with a quick burst of strength fueled by emotion, he fixed all senses on that animal and fought pain and wind and rain to reach it.

Battered by gusts that already had grounded the chopper and now bent the trees a third of the way over, he was glad, for once, that all those damned desserts over the years had given him the bulk to stay on his feet. Wincing, he came up at the shoulder of the kneeling Fowler and, without even a word, reached down and snatched the reins from his hand.

Fowler whirled to find him already digging a boot into the stirrup. "What the hell are you doing?" he demanded, clutching the stirrup leather.

L. D. swung on up and across, to excruciating pain in his knee. "I'm takin' it, Ernest!" he cried, kicking free.

Wheeling the animal, he gigged it with his one remaining spur and the mud began to fly across the veldt.

Through the rain ahead, he could make out only a hint of a figure that had to be Milton. Strangely, he suddenly dwelled more on his young deputy than he did even Charlie. For long hours now, everything had seemed out of L. D.'s control, as if he were powerless to do anything but wait for the gunshot that would leave Charlie draped over a horse. Maybe none of that had changed, as far as it concerned Charlie, but, damn it, Milton was up there acting crazy as hell and L. D. had to do something about it before the younger man got himself or somebody else killed. Hell, he'd hired him in the first place, so that made him responsible, in a way. He'd let all that hero worship play on his ego enough to pin a badge on him— and now he'd gone and put Milton in a situation where he just didn't belong.

In a lot of ways, L. D. knew, Milton was a good kid, but this kind of thing had just brought out the worst in him. And for Milton's own sake, if nobody else's, it had to end right here and now.

With his superior horsemanship, L. D. soon overtook the younger man and brought his horse abreast. They rode side-by-side through the howling storm for long seconds, yet L. D.'s eyes remained fixed on the suddenly dark grassland ahead, even when he knew Milton had turned to him.

Finally, L. D. looked straight into his eyes. "That's it, Milton," he shouted over the wind and thunder. "Your badge— soon as we get back in."

Then he spurred his animal ahead, leaving Milton to catch the flying mud.

L. D. had put five or six horse lengths between them when a tremendous explosion suddenly dropped his snorting horse to its knees. Crying out, L. D. flinched at an uncomfortable tingle and fell with the saddle, which somehow stayed under him even as his momentum threw his upper body across the animal's neck. He saw diffused light play against falling rain. A stifling odor like burning sulphur choked his throat, and his soaked shirt suddenly felt dry against his skin. God Almighty, lightning!

Immediately the addled horse struggled up with him, only to wobble around under his weight like a just-foaled colt. He knew he was lucky, damned lucky, but now he and Milton had to act fast or the next bolt would kill them.

"You all right, Milton?" he cried, wheeling his horse around.

L. D. saw and shuddered, forgetting his own predicament in the sudden shock that robbed him even of the sulphuric breaths burning his nasals.

Milton's horse, sprawled out dead as hell. And Milton, face-down in the mud off to the right and just as motionless.

"Milton!"

In seconds he was at his side and sliding off his horse to sprawl stiff-kneed before him. He could feel the raging wind and pummeling rain on his shoulders and see lightning's reflection play on the back of Milton's head. He slipped a hand down along the wet neck and found a weak pulse, then he took him by the upper arm and turned his head and shoulders out of the mud. He rolled him on over to his back and tried to use his own body to shield his face from the storm. Still, the rain came, sending muddy rivulets down the pale cheeks.

"How bad you hurt? You hear me? How bad you hurt?"

The eyelids quivered and the lips parted a little, letting in a stream of blood from a cut over the eye.

"Damn it, Milton, talk to me!" cried L. D., wiping away the blood with his forearm.

The lips were moving, slowly, silently.

"You gotta talk, Milton! You gotta let me know!"

He suddenly felt the younger man's hand clutching his shoulder, and as the lips continued to move, L. D. put an ear close enough to feel the warmth of his face. And when the words finally came, they were slow and raspy and hollow, the kind a scared, dying man might voice.

"I'm gone, L. D. I'm gone."

L. D. pulled back to look into his face, and quickly, all kinds of fear ran through him. "You're gonna make it—you hear me? *You're gonna make it!*"

The last word still was on L. D.'s lips when the younger man's hand fell away and he groaned to a sudden spasm that racked his body.

"Milton!" he cried, reaching for him and cradling the head that suddenly had fallen to one side. "Damn it, Milton, don't you go dyin' on me!"

There was one last breath, like air leaking out of a cattle truck tire, and then not even a frantic attempt at CPR there in the mud and wind and rain could make any difference.

Through the fog of crippling weakness, Charlie heard the ricocheting bullets and dug deep into his will for the strength to hang on to the faltering bay. With inner cries and raspy words, the whip of a hand and touch of spurs, he coaxed the gelding to find its own will to carry them on across the stormy tableland. He still clung stubbornly to the rifle, knowing it was his only chance but hesitating to profane the pristine wilderness with bloodshed by his own hand. Too, even though L. D. was hunting him down just like the two of them had done coyotes on the JAs, Charlie didn't like to think about suddenly finding L. D. down the sights.

The land, too, troubled him, for no longer did it merely whisper a hint to leave, it seemed to demand it in every crack of lightning and each howling gust. Already, the blowing sand that stung his eyes all but hid Green Mountain's ridge ahead, and now the rain was picking up, the drops beating out a somber rhythm on his hat and dripping off the brim.

Give it up, Charlie, you don't belong out here; you don't belong anywhere.

The voices suddenly seemed to come rolling out of the thundering clouds.

Your time's passed, Charlie; it was gone a hundred years the moment you were born.

He looked back through the falling rain to see the pursuing horseman gaining ground with every stride.

Can't you see it's all over for you, Charlie? Can't you see there's no place left to run?

He saw it, all right, but as the land turned dark under the growling clouds he again felt that benevolent spirit leading him on, now through a sudden wall of rain that seemed to stretch all the way to Green Mountain.

For long minutes that he knew must have been miles he pressed the bay through a battering downpour driven by powerful straight winds, until the turf grew so drenched that clods of mud flew with each dig of the animal's hooves. He looked back time and again through the furious storm to see a dim figure always gaining on him. Only a hundred yards of sheet-like rain separated them by the time the ground turned rocky and began to fall away, little by little, through cedars swaying ghost-like through the rain. The hooves clanged across exposed bedrock streaming with runoff and splattered a muddy chute, and even as Charlie took the horse sloshing on down through the rivulets he knew he had wrenched the bay even of its will.

They crashed through a wall of briars and went slipping and sliding down a final sloppy bank to the bed of an arroyo. He turned the horse downstream and the animal dropped knee-deep into the first of two rushing ditches snaking side-by-side. For a few frantic strides along its course, the bay splashed and lunged and struggled, then Charlie felt the legs give way and suddenly he and the animal both were down in the mud.

He lay on his hip in the far ditch, his right heel against the cantle and the impeded current crawling up his back and surging over his waist. He couldn't see his left leg for the muddy stream, but nobody had to tell him that a half-ton of horse flesh held it fast. What he didn't know was whether his boot was still in the stirrup—or whether the animal now struggling to rise had the strength to drag him.

But he'd be damned if he found out the hard way. Finding the reins still in his fingers, he quickly stilled the gelding by pulling its head around to its shoulder. He knew a pinned cowboy, even a weak one, could hold a horse down that way all day—but time was something that Charlie didn't have. There was a rider coming over the bank any second now, and he was going to shoot him dead just as surely as if he were a coyote in a trap.

So is this how it's all gonna end, L. D.? he asked silently. *With me just layin' here and somebody else makin' this water run red with my own blood?*

He thought about what his foster mother had told him, and about that little wind-swept grave out back of the old house in Walnut Canyon. He couldn't understand. He turned his face up into the falling rain and just couldn't understand.

He was going to die here, as cruelly as that little boy had all those years ago, and his whole life was going to end up just as meaningless.

He had come up from Cedarville, finally bearing hope inside, only to see it disintegrate before a haggard old woman's words and a couple of photographs. Then this wilderness had given its own hope, until the twentieth century had snatched it away again. Maybe deep inside, all right, he now carried that measure of the Creator's peace he had never known before, but to a cowboy twice denied a time and place, it didn't seem enough somehow. He had to get away; he had to stay out of that prison cell so he could keep on chasing those haunting dreams. He wouldn't ever be able to change the calendar, and he couldn't change himself, but maybe out there somewhere waited a sprawling, free land where a cowboy could ride at peace with himself and the world. If he could just make it over Green Mountain, reach those railroad tracks a few miles on the other side, maybe he would have a chance to know someday.

The only thing was, he was going to be dead in seconds if he didn't do something.

He saw a movement through the shielding brush, and lifting the rifle from the mud, he rested the barrel across the skirt of the saddle and waited.

Chapter Seventeen

L. D. had a lot of regrets as he pushed his horse on through the storm, but his deepest right then was that he hadn't waited a few more seconds to ask Milton for his badge. The kid had looked up to him, and for two whole years L. D. had accepted and even enjoyed it. And now, damn it, Milton was dead and his last memory of L. D. had been about that lousy badge.

But all that was over and done with; he'd never be able to change it. Meanwhile, up ahead, through the sudden, marble-sized hail hopping on the ground, there was still Charlie and a future yet to be written. And he'd be damned if he'd let it all take place without doing what he could.

Stripped of his hat by the fall, he buried his face alongside the horse's wet neck and, with the crook of his arm, tried to shield his head from the thickening hailstones. Still, he rode, fighting to control the horse crazed by the sickening thuds against its skull. L. D. made another slow hundred yards that way, enduring the battering against his shoulder and back. Then the hailstones grew to half the size of the saddle horn, hard white rocks falling furiously out of the western sky, and all he could do was dismount to grasp the cheek of the bridle and turn his frantic horse away from the storm. Moments after he huddled under its breast, he whirled to the faint *zing! zing!* of a rifle from somewhere ahead, then again there was only the thunder and wind and pound of hail against the ground.

He knew something had happened up there, something *bad*. Hell, he had to do something—now! And yet here he was pinned, fighting just to hold on to his maddened horse and stay out of the hail that could have split a man's skull.

Worry and anticipation prolonged every passing second, and the longer he crouched there the more protracted it all seemed. Finally the hail slackened, and, even as he took another beating from the sky, L. D. regained the saddle to spur the horse on through crunchy ground as white as a deep snow on the JAs. He cringed at a lightning blast that broke the storm's dusk and set the icy veldt sparkling before him. Hell, he was going to get killed out here, killed just as dead as Milton, and there wasn't a damn thing he could do about it except hug the saddle horn and pray a backslidden-Methodist's prayer.

He rode in dread that way on across the tableland to where it turned rocky under the ice and began to drop off gradually amid wind-whipped cedars. Pea-sized hail went with him, beating a brutal cadence on his shoulder and back. Where the brush thickened, his horse splashed down a slope streaming dirty-white with drift and hail, and they burst upon a rifle barrel thrusting out of the shadowy limbs to the left.

"Hold it! It's me!" he yelled, dodging and throwing a forearm up.

He saw the muzzle withdraw, and as he pulled rein he heard Syers' distinctive cursing and caught the shifting form of the ranger's horse through the swaying cedars. "Syers! What happened up here?" he cried above the furious wind.

He waited as the anxiousness and fear built, and even as Syers came up on foot out of the shielding cedars, the ranger still had only curse words, now directed at the pelting hail.

L. D. turned his horse toward him. "I asked you what happened!"

"The SOB," Syers snarled. He motioned with his rifle to the drop-off on down the slope. "Just when it began hailing so damned hard, bastard took a couple of pot shots at me."

"So there *was* some shots, right here close by you."

"You damned right there were. Wasn't for the hail bashing my brains in, I'd've killed the SOB."

L. D. found his eyes. "So what was it, Syers? What kind of rifle was it? If you were so damned close, what kind of rifle was it?"

Those hardened eyes narrowed. "Open your damned eyes and look at this stuff," he snapped with a sling of his head to the whitewashed ground. "Pounding down like hell, and wind blowing so loud we've got to stand here yelling at each other. And you hear that? That thunder and water running down there? And the air's so heavy you need a damned ax to cut your way through. It was a rifle, Hankins—that's all. And I'm damned lucky to be able to say *that* much."

L. D. breathed sharply and brought his horse up before him. "You know, don't you," he accused, staring straight into his eyes. "Deep inside, you *know*."

"Go to hell."

L. D. took a deep breath and turned his face back toward the veldt, and the frustration and anger built as he remembered. He whirled upon the ranger and began swinging off his horse. "Somethin' else, Syers," he snapped, finding the hail and mud under his boots and leading the gelding to within arm's reach of the man. "Somethin' else, *you son of a bitch*."

And with every ounce of his weight behind it, he drove his fist hard and twisting into Syers' teeth and jaw.

The impact numbed L. D.'s hand and jarred him right up to the shoulder, but it was the ranger who staggered back and fell to the mud. Stunned, he wallowed there, groaning and shaking his head like an old ram dazed after butting skulls with a rival. When he came to his senses after a few seconds and whirled to L. D. towering above, it was to unleash a torrent of invectives that culminated with his hand thrusting out for the Ruger, which lay just out of arm's reach.

"Just give me one little excuse, Syers!" cried L. D., making sure the ranger saw his hand at the grips of his holstered magnum. "Just one little excuse!"

Syers' arm relaxed, but the curse words only grew more hostile as he brought the back of his hand to his bloodied lip.

"You don't have no idea, do you!" continued L. D. "You went to shootin' so crazy that you don't have no idea! You stuck that barrel right out over my horse's ears and spooked the hell out of him till he throwed me, hung me up in the stirrup to where he liked to have drug me to death! You almost got me killed back there, shootin' at somebody that you know didn't kill Powers no more than me!"

The ranger spat a bloody stream. "You think I give a damn anymore what happened to Powers?" he cried. "That bastard's gone and shot at *me* now, and I don't *need* any more reason to bring him back belly-down on a horse."

L. D. turned and swung up on the gelding to glare down at him. "If Charlie had wanted you dead, you'd be dead right now."

And wheeling the horse down-slope, he kicked it in the belly to send mud flying back from the hooves. His hand was bleeding and it hurt like hell, but somehow, in every other way, he felt a damn lot better now.

The moment after Charlie fired two quick shots high up through the falling hail and turned the shadowy horseman away from the brushy bank, he set to work unbuckling the off-side cinches. He took a fierce beating from the sky as he did, but once they slipped free, he pulled the saddle on over into the rushing water with him and gave the horse the rein to turn its head from its shoulder. He clung tightly to the reins as the gelding struggled up, then held the hail-spooked animal while he disengaged his submerged boot from the stirrup gripping it fast. Gaining his feet with sheer will, he cast anxious glances back up the slope and used strength he didn't even know he had to hoist the muddy saddle across the horse's withers. He took time only to tighten the front cinch, then he somehow dragged himself up across the animal and they were off downstream through the pounding hail.

Draped forward over the saddle horn, he could only hang on as the weakened animal fought its way in and out of the surging channels cutting ever-deeper in the slippery loam. Before him, twigs and leaves came raining down from overhanging limbs thrashed by hail. He reeled with sickness and exposure to the storm, and the minutes were all but lost as the gelding carried him on between muddy banks streaming with runoff, and past small, rushing waterfalls at rock pouroffs. Finally, at a sharp bend to the right, a drift dam turned the horse up out of the water and through a slushy break in the left bank.

The bay wandered on, for minutes or hours, its hooves grating against layered hailstones that melted first to slush and then to mud. And slowly, like random pieces of a puzzle, the details of the terrain pierced Charlie's inner fog. The stumbling animal was taking him northeast through rough, broken country—not flats and canyons as before, but brushy badlands with many winding drainages, low bluffs sculpted from mud and sandstone, and small buttes standing at the forks of gullies rushing with water. And always, the rain pelted down, until Charlie rode shivering and his lucid moments grew more infrequent.

He heard the voices as he rode; they seemed to echo up out of a deep, black well, voices of gloom and despair and suicide.

It's time to end it all, Charlie, just like the Old West ended a hundred years ago.

He turned his wrenched face up into the falling rain and grieved for that place that should have been his, that should have been a cowboy's.

Don't you know your place is waiting for you, Charlie? Right there in that little grave in Walnut Canyon where you've always belonged?

He remembered the dust devil swirling across it, and the dark-suited man standing over the larger grave beside it and muttering something about there being some things that just weren't meant to be understood.

It's time to end it, Charlie.

Charlie, it's . . . time.

"Go to hell!"

His cry exploded out through the cedars and bluffs, and when it came echoing back he suddenly felt that benevolent spirit riding with him again, fighting all the dark, hopeless voices and alone giving him the will to go on. If he could just make it over Green Mountain, if he could just reach those railroad tracks, *if he could just get one more chance.*

Again, he drifted away into feverish oblivion and timelessness, and when his head cleared once more, he found his horse breaking through the wet brush and thorny vines alongside a torrent roaring out-of-banks and white with foam. Through the dripping leaves he saw its powerful currents, thick with silt and drift, tossing twigs and huge limbs alike in the all-consuming sweep downstream. Surging higher by the moment, it was an awesome force, and even though it was only a couple of horse lengths wide, Charlie didn't have to be an expert in flash flood hydraulics to know that even a fresh animal would stand no chance in it.

He looked away through viny oaks to his right and saw tiny streams falling down a mossy, limestone bluff springing up abruptly only yards away. It stretched on before him, an unbroken wall guarding the arroyo as far as he could see. Turning around in the saddle, he found a deluge free-falling the final fifteen feet from a pour-off rising up through a jumble of boulders and twisted roots. Splashing down as it did on bedrock back along the bay's course, the waterfall, Charlie realized, must have stirred him into awareness as the horse had carried him under it.

He rode on a few paces and the brush across the arroyo opened up to where he could look up through the rain and see a dark, bony ridge, only half a mile away, rearing before even blacker storm clouds. Across and to the left, and much nearer, lay a swell of bare land. The greenery at his face hid its summit, and he anxiously turned the horse a little, trying to make it out. Still, the leafy vegetation obscured, but by repeatedly shifting the animal, he finally pieced together a leftward-leaning slope angling sharply up to a great fist of rock, part of a hogback that stretched northward to the main ridge. With both sudden hope and despair, he recognized it as a jutting point of Green Mountain, hovering over him so tantalizingly close yet rendered, by floodwater, as distant as the black clouds beyond.

Green Mountain, the Comanche mountain of visions.

It stood, storm-wrenched and mysterious, as the final barrier between this profaned wilderness and those tracks, between one last cowboy's surrender to an uncaring world and his only hope for a tomorrow.

And somehow, he had to make it over it.

In the arroyo bed where Charlie's horse had fallen, L. D. found the churned loam and the trail of stirred and muddied hailstones leading away. He followed it down along the rushing ditches, and at a sharp bend he turned his horse up through a break in the bank to pass alongside the conspicuous can of beans, red-hued against white.

Rain alone pelted down now, and the rising runoff was carrying away the rapidly melting hail. Soon, L. D. knew, there would be no sign of Charlie's trail. But damn it, Syers was following back there somewhere, with his finger on the trigger, and somehow L. D. had to get to Charlie first.

For a long, brutal hour he tracked Charlie on through badlands more rugged than anything he had seen the past three days. His course carried him up and over thicketed fingers of land running out irregularly over a maze of flowing gullies, then down between their steep, winding banks and past forks guarded by muddy buttes. Sometimes, as the trail faded, he found horsehair clinging to a thorn, or a freshly broken limb or deposit of manure, but for the most part he counted himself lucky just to find the hint of a track here, the hope of one there.

He was glad when the maze finally was behind him; the thorns had bloodied his arms and all the up-and-down riding had aggravated his saddle sores. But now, in this elevated stretch of brushy cedars twisting up out of bedrock, he finally had to admit to himself that he had lost Charlie's trail. He slowed, leaning over to study the ground as the horse splashed through puddles and kicked little rocks along. He was searching for bedrock chipped by iron, a stone turned dirty-side up, a pulpy break in the cacti, anything to give him reason to go on through the damned storm that already had chilled him to the bone.

He straightened in the saddle to ease his aching back and saw it.

Eery fire danced at the tips of the horse's ears.

L. D. reined up in stunned silence, mesmerized by the flashes that seemed to start along the animal's neck and sweep up and out with a low crackling. Looking down, he found the same strange discharge on the rowels of his spur. He couldn't decide whether the color was misty purple, yellow-red, or bluish-green; at times it seemed to have hues of each. The horse seemed unaware, and L. D. couldn't resist passing his hand through it, without sensation.

He had heard old cowboy Tom talk about it on the JAs, how in the early days the lightning had danced on the horns of the cattle and become a ball of fire running down the mane of his horse to split at the saddle horn. Once, finding it playing on his six-shooter, Tom had even tossed the weapon in under a shrub and ridden away.

L. D. had discussed the phenomenon one time with the county agriculture agent; the official had called it Saint Elmo's fire, and explained it as a rare, luminous flow of electricity. L. D. didn't know about that, but he knew it was damned spooky no matter what a person called it.

The fire went with him on through the cedar brakes until he broke onto a rocky rim overlooking a gulch roaring with floodwater. Through a dead cedar, L. D. saw that the gulch dropped sharply before him, but on across the churning arroyo it rose gently to the base of a jutting hogback of Green Mountain.

Looking down through the canyon, he started at the sight of a horseman, moving slowly through the tangled greenery along the torrent's near side.

Chapter Eighteen

Charlie! Good God, it was Charlie!

L. D. whirled back up the west-trending rim to find its drop as sheer as that at the horse's breast, then wheeled the animal down-canyon into the timber fronting the rainy ledge. He had to find some way down! He had to get to Charlie, take him into custody, or Syers would show up and shoot the hell out of him! Good God, he had to *do* something—fast!

But the cliff remained unbroken, all the way through a brutal stretch of dead-limbed cedars that clawed at his arms.

He took the horse splashing into a film of water running down the concave slopes of a broad depression in the bedrock and reined up. He found himself at the head of a rushing pour-off, stair-stepping its way down into the gulch; below, he could count five or six solid-rock levels, each ending with inward-curving cataracts thirty feet wide and a few feet high, leading to a final waterfall crashing fifteen feet to a jumble of boulders. The bordering growth was especially heavy all the way down: oaks and elms thick with leaves, and big cedars with bare, twisted roots that hugged the bedrock.

It was an impossible descent for a horse, and bum knee and all, L. D. knew what he had to do.

He dismounted awkwardly to tie the gelding to a cedar and remove his leggings, then he was wincing and sloshing stiff-legged down through the runoff. The bedrock sloped more severely as he neared the first cataract, and before he knew what was happening, the current upended him and he went sliding on his hip off the first watery shelf. He dropped three or four feet to be swamped, then the strong, downward drive of the water carried him tumbling and sliding on down the chute.

He managed to sprawl back against the underlying rock and get his legs out in front just in time to ride the water over the next cataract. It spilled him another three feet to flood his face again, and as he glided away he gasped for air and fought harder to arrest his slide. But all he could do was control it, on over a third small cataract, down through another connecting trough, off still another ledge overhanging a chute. Surging out from under the falls he looked past his boots at the down-sweeping water and saw it abruptly disappear at the final pour-off only yards away. God Almighty, it was dropping fifteen feet to all those jumbled boulders, and he was flat on his back and headed straight toward it!

He suddenly thought about Sarah and all those damned dreams he had let slip by over the years, then about the cowboy who in the last three days had taught him how to fight like hell to keep a dream alive. And he turned to bury his face in the gushing water and scrape fingers and boot edges against rock all the way down the chute, until his legs went spilling out over the falls and his hand suddenly caught on a bulging root.

With a primal cry he clamped his other hand over it and just clung there, splitting the rushing water and fighting its powerful, downward pull against his dangling legs. He kicked for a foothold and found only empty space in under the pour-off, then all he could do was drag himself right-to-left across its face by means of the submerged root. He could taste the mud in the current and feel the rock lip scrape across his fleshy midsection, but finally he was close enough to a big cedar to seize its twisted bole and pull himself out of the water.

Still, he was in a precarious position; the cedar thrust up out of solid rock with no foot or hand holds, and below, the face sheared away left and right to slant in halves to the canyon floor and leave a jutting V down the middle. Shaky and weak, he turned immediately to the slope fronting the pour-off and slid on his buttocks on down through the spray to the boulders at the recessed base.

He suddenly thought about those two shots that earlier had turned Syers away, and he threw his back up against the tilted shield of rock and drew his .357 magnum. It abruptly occurred to him that it was the first time he had ever pulled the weapon in the line of duty—and he had done so now to level it on his best friend. But damn it, Charlie was a wounded animal out there, backed into a corner and now maybe dazed out of his senses, and L. D. owed Sarah more than to go sticking his head out like a prairie dog and risk getting it blown off.

Drawing the revolver up to his chest and finding its grips with both hands, he took a long, deep breath and whirled around the jutting rock to find greenery and Charlie down the barrel. He was thirty yards away, slumped over a wreck of a horse alongside the torrent. Relaxing his aim, L. D. limped on out from under the falls until his boots found the arroyo's muddy overflow and he had an unimpaired line of sight down between the dripping leaves.

"Okay, Charlie! I'm takin' you back in!" he cried above the din of the water.

He saw Charlie lift his head like a sick and injured man and look around; still, he lay slumped over the saddle horn.

"You hear what I say, Charlie? I'm here to take you back in!"

To Charlie, the words seemed to come whirling up out of a deep funnel, and he lowered his head to his hand and tried to clear the cobwebs, stop the world from swimming. Then awareness suddenly swept over him and he stiffened, tightening his hand on the rifle crisscross on the saddle.

"Throw it on down!" cried L. D., bringing the revolver's sights swinging up across the horse's rib cage. *"For God's sake, throw it down!"*

Charlie's eyes came into sharp focus on the magnum before they did anything else, bringing him up straight in the saddle, only to suffer another wave of dizziness. He fought it off to find L. D.'s eyes tense and pleading behind the barrel.

"The rifle, Charlie!"

Emitting a long, weary breath he didn't even think he had left anymore, the cowboy let the weapon slip free down the off-side of the saddle; it was all he had strength enough to do.

L. D. watched through the bay's legs as the rifle hit on the butt of the stock and fell forward into the arroyo. He hobbled on, until he was close enough to be heard without shouting, and winced at the sight of Charlie's bloody neck and shirt. "Damn it, you're hurtin' bad, aren't you, partner?"

The cowboy forced a thin smile and found slow, hoarse words. "Looks like you're gettin' along like an ol' cow with the creeps yourself, L. D." He nodded to the revolver. "You figurin' on usin' that thing on me?"

L. D. looked at it with embarrassment and guilt and lowered it. "Your mother's wrong, Charlie," he said, finding the holster. "Your aunt, she's a sick woman and she's wrong about ever'thing."

Charlie studied his eyes for long seconds, surprised at what L. D. seemed to know, then he let out another exhausted sigh of resignation and shook his head. "I seen it, L. D. I seen that picture, that little grave down there in Walnut Canyon. I been seein' it all just as plain as hell my whole damned life."

L. D. breathed sharply and glanced down to kick at the mud. "Damn it, Charlie, I know all you been lookin' for's a little peace in this world ever since you were old enough to fork a horse. But I guess sometimes that's just too much to want for." He nodded back toward the Divide. "We don't *have* to let it be like that though, partner. Come on back in with me, and when you get out I'll throw this damned badge away and you and me both will go find work on some ranch again, just like the old days."

Charlie shook his head; there was a lot of pain in his squinting eyes. "That ain't you no more, amigo. It never was, least, not like it was with me. 'Sides, you ain't takin' me back to rot in no jail cell any more. You might as well go ahead and shoot me right here and now, 'cause you ain't takin' me back."

"Hell, Charlie, I've got to, don't you understand? They're gonna *kill* you out here, if you don't die anyhow." He nodded to his oozing wound. "Look at your damned throat— it's bad, isn't it."

Charlie ran pale, trembling fingers up along his wet, sticky neck and his voice grew weaker, the words slower. "'Member on the JAs how we'd work from 'you can' till 'you can't'? Well, I'm just about at *can't*." He struggled for a deep breath and glanced across the floodwaters at Green Mountain's stormy ridge, then searched L. D.'s eyes. "If you care, compadre, if you ever did care, then all I'm askin' is you just let me turn and keep on ridin' till I find some place I belong."

L. D. groped for the right words; he felt so damned helpless, right here when he needed so desperately to help the best friend he'd ever had. He knew Charlie didn't have a fault any worse than just hanging on to all the old-fashioned ideals that, L. D. supposed, no cowboy of the nineteen nineties had any right to have. For God's sake, he had to *help* him! After all, he and Charlie were partners in the same dream, except that L. D. had let his vision die while the cowboy still held on doggedly to his, despite a lifetime of dark, crippling obstacles.

"Damn it, Charlie, you *do* belong, just as much as anybody."

Charlie shook his head weakly; he was beginning to drift away again. "You and me both know that just ain't so, amigo. A hundred years ago maybe, but not no more." He groaned from deep inside and slumped forward across the saddle horn so that his hat brim hid his face. "Just . . . let me ride on, L. D. Turn your back and just . . . let me ride on."

L. D. would never know what his answer would have been. The quick *pop! pop! pop!* of gunfire suddenly burst out over the roar of the arroyo to snap Charlie's arm forward and set the horse rearing and squealing. *What in the hell—*

L. D. whirled to lift his eyes up through the viny oaks rising against the cliff and found the cedary rim and the horseman against the stormy sky. Syers, the son of a bitch! L. D. spun back to see the blood on Charlie's arm and on the horse's hindquarter, then the cowboy was spurring the animal and pressing it down-canyon along the raging gully.

"No!" L. D.'s cry died in another quick *pop! pop! pop!*, and he looked back up through the oaks to see the horse jump forward along the rim as Syers kicked the animal in the belly. *"Syers, you bastard!"*

The ranger was taking the horse down-canyon right above Charlie! He was following along right at gulch's edge so he could pick him off through the next break in the timber! He was going to shoot him down just like he was a sheep-killing coyote, and there wasn't one damned thing in the world L. D. could do to stop it!

Still, he hobbled groaning with pain on after the lame, fleeing horse and its limp rider, and at the next volley he saw Charlie turn the bleeding animal into the greenery at the swollen bank. Another barrage cut a shrub at Charlie's shoulder in half, and as the limbs and leaves fell, he plunged the snorting horse into the raging floodwaters. They hit with a tremendous splash that impeded the flow and sent water surging far out of banks, then the current, striking broadside with overpowering force, rolled the horse and cut Charlie adrift.

"Charlie!"

L. D.'s cry was lost in the roar of the rapids that swept Charlie and the thrashing horse swiftly downstream. Charlie was groping for the saddle, fighting desperately for it, but the incredible rush of the water only drove him farther away. He suddenly went under in all the froth and drift and didn't pop up again for several yards and long seconds. Even then, it was only to go bobbing and struggling on through the churning waters downstream, until finally the muddy foam buried him and never let him up.

A silent cry exploded from the wellsprings of L. D.'s dreams. *Good God, you're drownin', Charlie! Charlie, you're drownin'! Drownin'! Drownin'!*

With a rush of adrenalin L. D. forgot all the pain and burst into as fast a run as his bum knee and eight years of soft living would allow. He broke through cracking limbs that whipped his arms, and tangled briars that grasped at his legs and set him stumbling. He fought his way on until his knee finally screamed with agony and he grew so weak and exhausted that he tripped over his own feet and fell hard to the rocky bank. Wheezing and groaning, he lifted his head to the arroyo and saw the unyielding water still churning on, and he knew that there was nothing else he could do.

He rolled over on his back and looked up through the dripping leaves, and the realization flooded him just like the falling rain did his face.

It was over.

Finally, it was over.

Drained in an instant of all strength and will by things that had nothing to do with the heave of his lungs or pound of his heart, L. D. could only lie there struggling for air and replaying it all in his mind. Only after long, crippling minutes, as dark as the clouds overhead, did he finally drag himself up weak-kneed and shuddering and see it in the froth.

Your hat, Charlie! Charlie, your hat!

It rode a thrashing limb that jutted out at water level from the near bank, and even though it offered despair rather than hope, he limped over to sprawl at gully's edge and reach for it.

He suddenly heard a cracking of brush from downstream and whirled to see Syers come riding up; somewhere down-canyon, the ranger had worked his way to the bottom of the gulch. And instantly all of L. D.'s pent-up emotions—the guilt and the rage and the grief—exploded into vicious epithets and a threatening move for his holster.

Syers brought the barrel of the .223 swinging down toward him, and an arrogant smile crossed his puffed, bloodied lips.

"Just back on off, you SOB," he snapped. "This show's all over now, so just back on off." He nodded downstream and laughed cruelly. "His horse is lodged up down there dead as hell—but not any deader than that bastard's got to be. He's probably washed halfway to the Colorado River by now." He made a swaggering sweep with his arm and looked at his wristwatch. "Say, if we hurry we can still make that hot little redhead's shift down at the cafe."

Turning away with a sharp breath, L. D. went ahead and reached for the hat and brought it out dripping, knowing that Syers was right, knowing that nobody in Charlie's condition could have possibly survived, knowing that he was submerged face-down and dead somewhere out in those churning waters.

Standing, he stared down at the soaked, misshapen brim and passed trembling fingers across the sweat stains, and didn't look up even when he heard Syers ride away.

Charlie was gone. *Gone!*

And with him he had taken the last of those dreams he had chased for both of them, dreams as foredoomed as a nineteenth century cowboy fighting a twentieth century world.

A great clap of thunder turned him a little up-canyon toward Green Mountain's jutting spur, and as he looked across the tossing foam and up through the leafy oak, he started as if someone had poked him with an electric cattle prod.

There, on that dark fist of rock backdropped by even blacker clouds, burned an eery, bluish outline, the outline of a man ablaze in Saint Elmo's fire, the outline of—

"*Charlie!*"

L. D.'s cry came only in a hoarse whisper, but it sent shock waves reverberating through his fiber until long after Charlie escaped over Green Mountain's main ridge.

Chapter Nineteen

Sunday, June 6–Tuesday, June 8
The days passed, and back in the county seat, L. D. didn't
break his silence even to Sarah. He kept quiet even as the
floodwaters subsided and Syers sent out troopers, and on
through the two days it took them to search the arroyo on
through the gulch and to its confluence with the Colorado
River. Through withdrawn days and wide-eyed nights he
could only think about Charlie and those awful wounds, and
wonder if he'd make it, and to where, and if he'd ever found
the peace he'd been looking for his whole damned life.

When the troopers came back in without the rifle, much
less Charlie's body, he worried that even if the cowboy still
were alive, it might not be over for him. He knew a vindic-
tive lawman like Syers wouldn't rescind the nation-wide
all-points bulletin without seeing a body bag first. And as
long as the country believed an armed and dangerous murderer of a Texas Ranger was on the loose, there was always
the chance that some panicky officer would stumble on him
somewhere and be too quick with a bullet.

But the most frustrating thing to L. D. was that he had
seen the rifle, across Charlie's saddle—and it had been a
twenty-two. But damn it, the one-sided stories Syers and
Fowler had brought back from the canyons had cost him his
credibility with the state police, and the only thing he could

do about it was sit around with his damned leg propped up and wait for those autopsy and ballistic reports to crawl back.

That, and say a prayer for Charlie and Milton.

Sunday, June 13
From the open door of a slow-moving boxcar, Charlie dropped to the gravel to face a high wall of stationary hoppers and tankers only a few feet away. Through his split-and-laced boots, he could still feel the vibration of the clattering wheels as they rolled on behind him, creaking across a loose rail that sagged with the passing tons. He turned at the blare of an air horn and looked down the long, narrow canyon defined by the freight cars, and twitched at the sudden whiff of diesel smoke drifting back from the locomotive.

It was not a wilderness. It was not the eighteen hundreds. It was not a cowboy's place. It was the San Bernardino, California, freight yards, judging by the sign he had seen back up-track.

Eight days had passed since the storm. For Charlie, it had been eight days of huddling feverish inside weaving boxcars and watching through open doors as the Trans-Pecos crags, New Mexico badlands, and Arizona deserts had swept by. They had been days of fighting the fire in his neck and bullet-creased arm, of lying up weak and hungry in hobo jungles, of rummaging through dumpsters just for enough food to keep him alive.

Still, as he began stumbling weakly down the shadowy corridor, leaving behind a thousand miles of rail and haunting memories, he held on stubbornly through sheer will and his bulldogged hopes that his place waited for him somewhere ahead, always ahead.

The farther he trudged, the more the walls seemed to squeeze in on him, though they remained at arm's length on either side. They were choking him, just like the twentieth century always had done, just like their upper rims, in angling toward one another in the distance, choked the sunset sky. Finally, the sight of a brakeman far ahead turned him through the line of empty cars and on through an ensuing maze of gondolas, tankers, and boxcars. Across the last side track, a pasture overgrown with dead weeds and shrubs immediately drew him. But even as his boots found dirt, his loathing for the slums just a few hundred yards away drove him further down the line.

The rasp of weeds against jeans went with him until he paused near the railroad overpass that crossed north-to-south over the rails. Then the smell of a wood fire turned him into the pasture, and soon he struck a well-beaten trail that led him to a littered hobo jungle with cardboard shanties, old tires, and discarded refrigerators.

At a small campfire, a shirtless man with tattoo-blackened arms stood bent over, stirring the coals with a stick. Beyond the rising smoke, two other bums—one sickly thin and bruised at the cheek, one craggy-faced and swollen at the jaw—sat passing a bottle of cheap wine. On a length of cardboard before a stack of tires, a fourth man, with greasy pants and dark, scraggly whiskers, lay with legs stretched toward the fire; Charlie could see the balls of his feet through the worn soles of his shoes.

"Got a cigarette, amigos?" Charlie asked wearily.

The man at the fire half-lifted his head; he bore a cut on his lip and an ugly bruise under his eye. "Hell, we ain't got *nothin'*," he slurred. "Done took ever'thing we had last night, thanks to that damned little runt over there." He motioned across the fire with his head.

Caught in mid-guzzle, the sickly bum left wine dribbling down his chin in his haste to respond. "Don't go blamin' me—you's the one followed me right in that joint."

"Yeah? Well, what sawed-off stump was it went flashin' his money 'round in there, jes' gettin' a stinkin' beer?"

The sickly man wiped his chin with the back of his hand. "Soon's I got back to the table, I *tol'* y'all they's up to somethin'. When we got up to go, I *tol'* y'all they's followin' us."

"'Bout caved my jaw in," whispered the craggy-faced man through teeth like broken slats in a fence.

The bum at the fire cursed vehemently. "Run a damned jackhammer all week and end up nothin' to show for it but a bunch of blisters. I'll cut their damned heads off next time." He straightened, a little unsteadily, and glared at Charlie. "What the hell *you* want?"

Charlie found a deep breath and glanced around, taking in the dusk streaking the sky red through the overpass. He thought about that little grave and the wilderness canyons, about what life had always been for him and what it should have been, and he knew that whatever it was he wanted, he would never find it here. Maybe in Mexico . . . Canada . . . Alaska . . .

He already had half-turned to the trail when the grease-streaked man, swigging from a bottle as he sat up, gestured toward him.

"Funny lookin' boots—where can I get me a pair like 'em?" he asked with tongue thickened by whiskey. Then a terrible scowl masked his face, and he dragged himself up to stand tottering, and glared with hard, bloodshot eyes. "Hey, don't he look kinda like one of them SOBs to you? That a billfold stickin' outa your back pocket, buddy? Where'd you get that thing? You 'member the one with the beard? You in that beer joint last night, you son of a bitch?"

Charlie felt so damned weak, he couldn't have lifted his fists if he'd wanted to. "Settle down, amigo," he said quietly, turning wobbly and exhausted to walk away into the horizon and tomorrow.

But suddenly, four slurred and agitated voices rose behind him.

"You see the whiskers on his face? The way his shirt's all tore up and bloody? 'Member me knockin' the hell out of one of 'em?"

"Hey you! You got our money in that billfold? Gimme that thing!"

"He the one stood over me, kickin' me and laughin'? He the one kicked me and laughed? The SOB, he look like the one?"

"Hell, he's close enough, ain't he?"

Turning from the burnt orange sunset, Charlie saw four scowling men stumbling toward him out of the swirling smoke.

Moonrise that night found a shadowy figure staggering toward a northbound train that barreled down off the overpass and through the freight yards. With the approach of a flat car loaded with a truck trailer, the figure began moving with the wheels that clicked across joints in the rails. The car easily overtook the form and began surging by, the couplings front and back banging taut in quick succession. The trailing ladder came even, and at the last instant the stumbling figure lurched toward the fleeing rungs.

The ladder swept on by, empty, and then there was nothing but the roar of the wheels and the long, lonesome howl of a whistle.

Friday, June 18

Sitting sagged at his desk in the sheriff's office, L. D. massaged tired, aching eyes and stared again at the reports strewn before him.

Post-mortem. Ballistic. Veterinary. One by one, they had crawled in, and now that he had them all after two stressful weeks, he felt so emotionally drained that he didn't have energy even to sit up straight anymore.

The evidence was conclusive—Charlie was not a murderer. A parole violator and a horse thief, yes, in the view of the law, but not a murderer.

For the dozenth time, he thumbed through the reports: the post-mortem, showing the entry and exit wounds in Powers' neck to be consistent with a high-speed bullet such as a .223, and the veterinary and ballistic, establishing that the colt had died from a .22 caliber slug discharged from a rifle, not a pistol. At the head of that canyon, Charlie had fired a twenty-two rifle—not a Ruger .223. Even without .223 fragments from Powers' body to implicate Syers' weapon directly, the responsibility for the killing clearly had shifted from Charlie to the ranger.

Charlie was as innocent as L. D. in the killing of Powers, and yet they had hunted him down and shot him just as if he had been an animal. And, damn it, L. D. knew he was more to blame than anyone, regardless of how he had tried like hell to stop it. For it had been he, and he alone, who had looked upon the theft of a horse and seen cause for a manhunt.

Why the hell couldn't I have just left you alone, Charlie? he cried silently, as he had day and night for thirteen long days now. *Hell, you wasn't askin' for so much, was you—just the right to be left alone to ride the way a cowboy ought to. All you was wantin' was just a little peace, and I couldn't let you alone.*

Even at the end, when he'd had a chance to make it up to Charlie, he hadn't been able to find the courage and conviction to do as the cowboy had pleaded and just let him ride away. Maybe it would have been wrong in the eyes of the law, even wrong in a humanitarian sense, considering Charlie's wound. But, damn it, for the sake of all those dreams they once had shared, maybe he'd owed it to the cowboy and to himself.

Out of the stacks of papers the phone suddenly was ringing. He let it ring. He didn't want to talk. He didn't want to deal with anyone. All he wanted was another chance with Charlie.

But the ringing contraption in front of him just wouldn't go away. He breathed sharply and began turning to look across the office. Hell, why didn't Milton pick up the damned thing?

Milton.

He saw the empty desk and a half-laugh choked his throat with guilt and grief. Hell, if he started asking for second chances, he didn't know how high he'd have to count.

He picked up the line, and on the other end was a fast-talking man who identified himself as a detective lieutenant with the San Bernardino, California Police Department.

"We've got your man out here," said the detective, "this Lyles fellow you been looking for."

"You what?" asked L. D., suddenly straightening.

"Yeah, this Charles Lyles. You put out an APB on him, didn't you?"

L. D. scooted back his chair and stood on his stiff knee. "I did early on; I put one out and then the Texas Rangers did."

"Well, we've got him—he's dead, run over by a freight train."

L. D. started, sudden dizziness setting him reeling. He reached for the desk to steady himself with trembling fingers, and a terrible chill swept down his shoulder blades. "He's . . . dead," he repeated lowly, strangely conscious of the sound of his own hoarse words.

The detective chuckled. "*I'll* say he is—he's all mangled to hell, hasn't even got a face anymore. Cut off one leg, a hand, part of another leg. Those tracks were a bloody mess up and down there for a hundred yards."

L. D. shuddered, and the receiver began quivering at his ear. "You . . . know it's him," he said, still barely above a whisper.

"Found his billfold, a Texas driver's license. That's what we're going on, that and dark hair, big build. Body's so torn up, that's as close to a positive ID as you're ever going to get."

"Fingerprints," muttered L. D. "You got fingerprints."

"I'm barely making you out. Can you talk any louder? You say prints? Nothing left. Not even enough for a dental record check. A freight train run over you and drag you down the tracks the way that one did, that's what's going to happen."

L.D. clutched the phone cord with his free hand and fought the lump in his throat. No. He couldn't accept it. A cowboy wouldn't die that way. A cowboy *shouldn't* die that way. Charlie had found some way to get out of it, just like he had when they'd cut those trees in half with their bullets, just like he had when those churning waters had swallowed him. He'd found some way to keep on going and searching and dreaming, because it just wasn't fair that a cowboy like Charlie shouldn't. Damn it, Charlie still had to be out there!

"So you're not . . . *sure*," he said with a quiver.

"We're satisfied out here on *our* end. If you're up to your butt in cases anything like us, might as well mark it off your books and let it go at that."

"But scars, tattoos," pressed L. D. "What about tattoos? He had some, both shoulders."

"Hell, he's just raw hamburger, like I said. You can call the coroner and talk to him yourself if you want to, but you won't find out anything I haven't already told you. Nothing to make him stand out but his boots."

L. D. flinched and squeezed the phone cord until his fingernails dug into his hand.

The detective chuckled and went on. "Funniest thing I've ever seen. He'd taken a pair of cowboy boots and cut them down the front and laced them back up. Ever hear of anything like that?"

L. D. swallowed hard and slowly sank into the chair. "Yeah," he said with choked voice, "yeah, I have."

Chapter Twenty

Friday, June 25

All during the hot drive home from the funeral in Greenleaf, L. D.'s emotions rose and fell just like the shovel of that backhoe in Charlie's grave. Deep inside, all right, he knew that Charlie now had found maybe the only peace he ever could have, yet he felt guilt a thousand times worse than before.

At the end, all Charlie had wanted to hear from him had been a simple "Keep on ridin'," and he just hadn't been able to say it. Hell, hadn't he owed the cowboy that much, knowing all the things he'd had to grapple with his whole damned life? Hadn't he owed the best friend he'd ever had that much?

He had let him down, just like the whole damned world always had, and now, he would have to live with it the rest of his life.

Tugging at the stubborn tie that had choked him all afternoon, he went in the back door, draped his suit coat across a kitchen chair, and headed for the refrigerator and a beer.

"L. D., that you?"

He popped the tab of a cold Lone Star and took a swallow. It seemed to hang where the knot of the tie squeezed his throat. But even as he slipped the damned thing free and tossed it on the table, the knot still wouldn't go away.

Sarah met him at the living room door; her face was a little pale, and her fingers trembled as she brought her hand to his upper arm.

"Well, we got him buried," he said simply.

"Did you see him, L. D.? Did they let you see him?"

He took a long, deep breath and shook his head. "Closed casket." He patted her hand where it rested on his arm and brushed on past into the living room. "Had to, the way he was tore up."

"They send his billfold back with him? His boots?"

L. D. stopped before the coffee table and rubbed his tired eyes with a thumb and index finger. "Got 'em in at the office couple of days ago. Never knew anybody but Charlie to cut and lace a pair of boots the way he done."

Again, he felt Sarah's hand on his arm, and he turned to her with a deep sigh of resignation. "I'm so damned tired, Sarah. I'm just so damned tired."

She looked down, turning her head to one side to pass trembling fingers along the loose strands of hair at her temple. "Darlin', I . . ." She looked up at him and breathed deeply, lines of confusion suddenly at her eyes. Then again she lowered her head to let those quivering digits play along her temple.

He placed a caressing hand against the back of her hair. "Hey, what's wrong, anyhow?"

With a deep breath she found his eyes. "I got a call while you was gone, L. D., some man askin' for you."

He breathed sharply. "Another damned reporter? They was even out at the cemetery."

She shook her head. "He kind of talked in a drawl, real hoarse. When I told him you wasn't here, he said tell you somethin' for him."

"Yeah? What the hell was it all about?"

"He said, 'Tell L. D. that Charlie called—and I'm not dead.'"

L. D. stiffened and stared into her eyes.

"That's all he said," she went on. "And then he hung up, just like that. It was just a crackpot, wasn't it, darlin'? You were a pallbearer; you just buried him. That *was* him you buried, wasn't it, L. D.?"

L. D. remembered the dreams of two cowboys—one a would-be cowboy and the other a real one. He thought about the manhunt, and the turmoil of pitting his sense of duty against his admiration for a person unafraid to chase those impossible dreams both of them had shared. He thought about the hand that life always had dealt Charlie, and the frustrations and hopes that had driven him on in search of the peaceful, free land that should have been a cowboy's from the start. And still he looked Sarah straight in the eyes.

"He's dead and buried, Sarah," he said quietly.

He turned away to find the front screen door and stepped out on the covered porch. His eyes fell on his hand-made boots, lying beside the pillar at the top of the steps just as he had dropped them far into that stormy night three weeks ago. Unblemished throughout long months in a world in which he had abandoned his dreams, they now were caked with mud, and the uppers flopped to one side. At last, they were a *cowboy's* boots, even though he knew he would never wear them again.

Then he lifted his eyes higher, up through the breaks in the white, frame houses to the west, on to the green canyons and bluffs of the Divide drainage, and beyond to the red-streaked sunset. And with a nod and a knowing smile, he finally found the words, quiet against the background chirp of crickets, and filled with tomorrow's promise.

"Keep on ridin', Charlie."

Author's Note

Charlie Lyles, his relatives, lawmen, and all other characters in this novel are purely fictitious. However, certain incidents were inspired by an actual horseback-helicopter manhunt in Texas in the 1970s and an ensuing train-pedestrian fatality. I also drew extensively upon my interviews with seventy-four cowboys of early-1900s Texas and New Mexico.